LET ME TELL
YOU A STORY

LET ME TELL YOU A STORY

A COLLECTION OF WRITINGS

CHARLES KEITH HARDMAN

ARCHWAY
PUBLISHING

Archway Publishing books may be ordered
through booksellers or by contacting:

Archway Publishing
1663 Liberty Drive
Bloomington, IN 47403
www.archwaypublishing.com
1-(888)-242-5904

Because of the dynamic nature of the Internet, any web
addresses or links contained in this book may have changed
since publication and may no longer be valid. The views
expressed in this work are solely those of the author and do
not necessarily reflect the views of the publisher, and the
publisher hereby disclaims any responsibility for them.

Any people depicted in stock imagery provided
by Thinkstock are models, and such images are
being used for illustrative purposes only.
Certain stock imagery © Thinkstock.

ISBN: 978-1-4808-0548-4 (sc)
ISBN: 978-1-4808-0549-1 (e)

Library of Congress Control Number: 2014932203

Printed in the United States of America

Archway Publishing rev. date: 2/19/2014

CONTENTS

INTRODUCTION

I NEVER FORGOT THE STORIES that I wrote in the early sixties and for some reason I saved them for over forty years. I grew up watching the Twilight Zone and The Alfred Hitchcock Hour on a television that had a round screen that was powered by tubes. All the programs were in black and white and I waited for these shows to air like a heroin addict would look forward to his next fix. I wanted to believe that there was a world that couldn't be explained by my parents and could not be taught in any school. I wrote some stories that only Science Fiction Magazine and a few mystery magazines might publish at the time. I was a boy in his twenties that no one had ever heard of so I had no chance of anyone taking my writings as serious. I doubt if the magazines that I sent them to even read them. I accepted this fact with understanding and innocence. I wasn't a Rod Serling or an Alfred Hitchcock. I did save these stories and added a few more. I am now going to edit them to the present day and let the next generation judge them. Nobody expected a future like this one. Read my forty year old stories and rethink what could have been. I wrote these stories because there can be no boundary when a writer uses his or her imagination. There is only the unknown and that is where I am coming from and I hope to find in the future. Let me tell you a story. I don't think you have heard this one before? Just remember things were different in the sixties. I am editing them from the sixties. Just read them!

CROSSROADS ICEHOUSE

I WAS DRIVING MY LIME green Corvair on a long and lonely Texas highway somewhere near the panhandle. I had just been evicted from my apartment in Lubbock. This was actually a godsend. I couldn't have lived another day there anyway. I tried making a name for myself there by playing guitar and singing in dumps like Mario's Pizza and Italian Restaurant on weekends and any other place where the owners would pay me to try and bring in the students from the college. Let us just say that I failed to get any appreciation, or anything else for that matter in Lubbock. I had about $75.00 and a jar of change that I had collected from my gigs. If ever the phrase "two bit joint " applied to a place then I worked it. If it weren't for the college kids, even those dumps wouldn't classify as two bit joints. When you are down to working for tips in places that you would avoid most days then I was positive it was time to move on. I knew I had some self-respect left and Lubbock was not going to make me happy.

I left Lubbock and didn't really care where I was headed. I just knew that I had to leave. I was glad to see Lubbock in my rear view mirror. I pushed the gas pedal down and watched as the Texas red clay dust evaporated behind me. I was going somewhere. It didn't matter where, but it had to be better than what I was leaving. Nobody in the music business ever made it big by staying in one place. Especially in a place called Lubbock. I was screaming "Fuck It" as I pressed the gas pedal down as hard as I could.

I played the old time blues. I respected the black musicians that created this type of music. They didn't do it for money, they lived for the music they created. Now it was my turn to live for the blues. I had to move on because I could not make any more music in Lubbock. I was now on the road.

I looked at the red clay highway in front and behind me and knew it had to be leading me somewhere. Where I had been was just that. I figured that I must be getting close to becoming a bluesman because I had to move on. I think that is what makes a person play the blues. When it is all they have left in life. I pushed the gas pedal down as hard as I could. I never wanted to see what I left behind again. I was free for the first time in my life. Where I was heading was a song that hadn't been written yet.

I saw some lights up ahead of me. I took my foot

off the gas pedal and slowed down. It was getting dark now and and I was having a hard time focusing on the road. Endless nothing was what people called the roads in North Texas. They labeled them as routes, but they were more like roads to nowhere. They seemed endless. I was on one of them now. I saw white tents ahead. I was sure that they had ice chests filled with cold beer. It was an icehouse. Texas was famous for them. I knew that I had to stop. The icehouse was my next destination.

I pulled into a parking lot and turned off the ignition. I opened the door and stood on crushed oyster shells. I was nowhere near an ocean, but I knew the smell of one. This was no regular icehouse. I was going to find out where this road was leading me. I walked into the tent.

I saw rusting old coolers and no one attending them. I took a Lone Star longneck from one of the coolers and moved over to a bottle opener attached to a piece of string. I popped the top and spoke. "I want to pay for this beer. Is there anyone here?"

The place seemed deserted. I could see that the sun was beginning to set and it would be getting dark very soon. Just then a row of coolers lit up with bare light bulbs coming to life on what seemed to be christmas light strings. A radio started blaring behind the coolers. Then I saw him. He was an old man sitting in a wooden rocking chair. He just stared at me. I was frozen in his gaze. He then spoke.

"Welcome to the Crossroads Icehouse. The first beer is on the house."

He was kind of creepy looking and I couldn't even guess his age. He just sat there rocking and staring at me. He wore a straw hat, the kind negroes in the old south wore. He had a full mouth of teeth and smiled wide to show them. They were so bright that they sort of gleamed or twinkled in the light of the bare bulbs. His eyes were a muddy brown, the color of blood.

He wore blue jean coveralls and was barefoot. I couldn't tell if he was black or white or a little of both. His full attention was on me though. He seemed to be trying to read my thoughts. I felt uncomfortable and had to speak.

"I thank you for the beer. It seems empty in here. Is this usual for this time of day?"

He just rocked and stared at me. He was in no hurry to answer me. I was feeling scared and couldn't help but shiver. It was as if someone had walked on my grave.

He stared straight at me and said, "Not too many people stop here during the daylight hours. It seems most people that stop here are on there way to some-place else and don't need or want what The Cross-roads Icehouse has to offer. After the sun goes down though, people seem to need what this place has to offer."

He was now really creeping me out.

"We got a band that plays music every night. It seems to give the needy folks a place to come to escape whatever is making their lives so unfulfilled and futile. Kinda like bringing moths to a flame,"

I was now feeling that I was standing on ground that only the damned could stand on. He sat there staring at me with those bloody eyes trying to read my mind. I felt like he was trying to get inside my head. I took a long drink on the long neck and then looked into his eyes.

He just sat there rocking like he had nothing better to do for eternity.

I felt like time was standing still. Not one car had passed us by in over thirty minutes. I finished the beer and took out my wallet to pay for it.

"Like I said earlier the first beer is on the house."

He just kept rocking and staring at me with those bloody eyes.

"I thank you for the beer but I think I must be on my way. Are you sure that you don't want any money if I am not going to have anymore beers?"

"You are welcome at The Crossroads Icehouse. If you feel needy or are just a little curious, the band will start playing one hour after the sun goes down. Sometimes they let people sit in, that is if it is someone that wants to join the band."

I was getting spooked. The man was really starting to scare me. Something told me that I had to ask him how he knew that I was a musician. I know he never saw my car or guitar. I had to know how he knew.

"How do you know that I am a musician?"

He just kept rocking and seemed to see through me. He chuckled and stopped rocking.

"It is not what I know or don't know. It is what made you stop at the icehouse that is important. You could have kept driving past it. You stopped and had your free beer. You can leave or stay to hear the band. You are welcome at The Crossroads Icehouse. The band will start playing at one hour after the sun goes down."

I set down my empty long neck and started to leave. The old man spoke.

"Remember this, the first beer is always free at the Crossroads Icehouse. Once you have had your free beer you will always be welcome. Continue on your journey wherever it may lead you "

He just sat there staring at me and smiled a toothy grin that made me shiver.

I saluted him with a wave of my hand and walked toward my Corvair. I looked back , I noticed the old man was rocking again. He was staring straight ahead, it was like he was looking into the dusk for something.

I got into the Corvair and started to wonder what had just happened to me. When I stopped at the icehouse, I had no expectations. I may have been curious, or I just might have been in no hurry to get anywhere. Meeting the old man was very different from anything I had encountered in my life. I did choose to stop and now I was curious. As strange as the old man was, he was not offering me anything that I wasn't ready to accept. I decided to stick around and listen to the band.

It was getting dark now. I didn't know when one hour after the sun went down was but I knew it had to be soon. The old man was still just rocking and looking into the distance. He was still there but now he was standing and smoking a hand rolled cigaret. He turned his gaze upon me and spoke. "Beers are a dollar and there is no limit."

I had a strange feeling about the old man and the icehouse, but I was also very curious about both of them. Nothing I had experienced before was remotely like what I was feeling now. It was as if I was under hypnosis or in a trance.

"The band will start playing one hour after the sun goes down." The old man turned away from me and walked toward a make shift stage next to the icehouse. He was in no hurry and seemed oblivious to the fact that I was even still standing there. I took another longneck, dropped a dollar on the cooler and followed the old man to where the stage was set up. There were no musical instruments on the stage or any band members hanging around it. There were no seats for an audience either. The old man reached the stage and then turned and gave me another toothy grin. I heard gravel crunching. I turned to see pickup trucks and other vehicles pulling off the highway. It was just like the old man said, people were coming to the icehouse like moths to a flame. When I turned back around as if by magic there was a band set up on the stage. I took a long pull on my longneck and moved to a spot facing the center of the stage. I wasn't sure what was happening but I was just curious enough to stick around and find out.

The band struck its first chord and the sound was incredible. A saxophone played like it was Hell-bound. The lead guitarist stroked the strings on his guitar like it was on fire and also headed for Hell. The bass was emitting flames from its strings. The drummer was sending sparks flying everywhere. The second guitarist wasn't playing rhythm but was another lead. The audience was going wild. They felt the music. It seemed to entrance them. The music was intoxicating to me. Everyone was dancing and seemed to become part of the music. The music owned the audience. No one would leave disappointed. The sparks flying around the drummer was like a fireworks display that had been coordinated just for the music. More trucks and vehicles pulled off the highway and the audience seemed to double in size. I went back inside to get another longneck. The old man was sitting in the rocking chair again. He stopped rocking and turned and stared at me like he wanted to see my soul.

"You stayed to see the band but the band is here to see you. I can see you want to be a part of the band because you have been a one man band for too long. The band can play forever but soon they will need a new lead guitarist. The old one is over 200 years old and his contract is just about to end. You can become the new guitarist but you will have to become a new person. You will have to join the band. Are you ready to sign a contract?"

The old man was creeping me out. He was right about me wanting to be a lead guitarist in a band because I was going nowhere by myself. I could use this gig but if the old man wasn't just yanking my chain he had said that the old lead guitarist had been with the band for 200 years. I had failed as a solo artist so far and then I thought about where this gig would take me.

I felt like the old man was pressuring me. This was just a stop on the side of an endless highway in Texas. I wanted Las Angeles or San Francisco. "Fuck you old man! I am going to Los Angeles. The highway leading there is better than the Hell that you offer me here. If this roadhouse is all you have to offer me then it will have to continue without me. I need the limelight. Los Angeles is my next stop. Get another fool to be your lead guitarist. I refuse your free beer. Here is my dollar."

I tossed the dollar at the old man and got in my Corvair and drove away from The Crossroads Icehouse as fast as I dared. It sort of just disappeared in my rearview mirror. I somehow knew that I had just beat the devil. I was going to Los Angeles and play in some bars that didn't smell like burning mesquite wood.

THE IMPOSTOR

"ALL RIGHT, NOW THAT EVERYONE has had their chance, I will now tell you who I am."

These were the words that the town of Jamestown and the rest of the world were waiting to hear. This is what happened.

The mystery of what was taking place in the town of Jamestown had gotten everyone in the town, the state, and the nation involved. A stranger had come into the town of Jamestown on the night of the 5th of May and in a period of two weeks had managed to stay unknown or known as someone different to almost everyone in the town. Now how this happened wasn't really a mystery, but what happened to everyone in the town was. The stranger started at one end of the town and introduced himself to everyone that he met. What was so strange was that he introduced himself to each person as a different person. Jamestown was not a large town and the word got spread around that there was a stranger in town. What the town didn't understand that by introducing himself as a different person to each person he met he had almost doubled the town's population. He was Bill Reed to one and then Mike Nelson to the next. He also gave each person a different reason for entering the town. Soon the town was buzzing, for the prospect of having so many new people wanting to start businesses in town was a godsend.

Now how this stranger kept from being discovered as just one person so quickly was very tricky indeed. He stayed away from the center of the town where it was most populated, and if he came upon a person that that he had already met he remembered who he told them he was and why he had come to Jamestown. He managed to do this quite well for two days. Then the townspeople began to get suspicious because their businesses were not getting any new income. The town called a meeting and wanted the new person in town to attend it. He showed up and said that he wanted to remain anonymous.

This made the townspeople angry and they wanted him to reveal to them who he really was. He stuck to the story that he wanted to be anonymous, so they threw him into a jail cell. This just made matters worse. Everyone that he had introduced himself to thought that they knew who he was. The town couldn't get back to normal until they found out who this stranger really was. He had no identification on him and his clothes had no labels for them to figure out where he had come from. In fact, he had no money on him. He had been brought meals from different people each day that he was in town and no one knew where he spent the night. The kids in town loved all the excitement and soon the jail became the most popular spot in town. Everyone wanted to become the first person to discover who the stranger was.

His picture was sent to all parts of the state and even the surrounding states. His fingerprints were sent to Washington DC because he had to be on someone's radar.

Betting on who the stranger was became a business. This stranger had wife against husband and brother against brother. The town started staying open 24 hours a day and no one could maintain a normal schedule. Everyone was looking at his or her neighbor as a different person now. It was now hard to tell what Jamestown was like before this stranger showed up. When he entered their lives they changed so much that they were not the person that they were before he showed up. They were realizing how out of touch with the rest of the world Jamestown had become.

When the newspaper reporters and law enforcement agencies from other parts of the state began showing up, the town changed even more. Everyone in town had a story to tell about the stranger. They became celebrities. They posed for pictures with the stranger and each told a story about how they were trying to get the stranger to tell them who he really was. Some of them even lied and said that the stranger confided to them who he really was.

The reporters and law enforcement agencies just pressed harder to discover who this man was?

His identity was still a mystery after every inquiry came back as just another dead end.

Rewards were now being offered. The stranger was now only being seen by appointment. He was given new clothes, especially tailored for him. He was now known as the unknown gentleman by the newspapers and press. He still had no name that anyone could stick on him. He was invisible to the world except in Jamestown. Fights broke out over what to call him. Everyone thought they knew his identity by who he introduced himself to them. Women propositioned him, he was offered land, money, and even a political office position. He still said he wanted to stay anonymous.

After two months of pampering the stranger with food, clothing, and gifts the town decided to hire ruffians to beat the truth out of him. Many in the town were against this action, but since even all the law enforcement agencies and media couldn't find out who he was, they gave their approval.

The ruffians entered his cell and began beating him. The stranger still said that he was not going to talk. They tortured him, and then the town had to watch as he cried out in pain. After several hours of torture the townspeople circled him and asked him to tell them who he was?

That was when the stranger did something totally unexpected. He stood and faced the town.

"All right everyone has had their chance. I will tell you the truth now."

He walked over to his cell and collected his belongings. He started walking out of this cell and spoke very loud so everyone could hear him.

"I am an impostor."

SPACE FARE

SPACE HAS ALWAYS BEEN ONE of man's greatest inspirations. Mankind has always taken a keen interest in the unknown spaces that some call heaven and others just call outer space. Then there are those that look up and wonder what is up there? Still no race of people, or empire for that matter, could ever just let it alone. It is in our artwork, architecture, and in the dreams of our children. So, when the first space testing stations were formed, it was no wonder that every nation wanted to share the unknown spaces above us. That is why the meeting to not admit three nations to the use of these testing sites caused a world controversy.

It was a slap in the face to three countries of the world. This made these countries out of outer space. It meant that they were being denied something that every other country in the world had access to. This was a chance to share a future in outer space. These

three countries were being allowed to send a representative to try and understand why they had not
been included in what every other country had been
given access to. They demanded to be given a chance
to enter the space race. Their representatives were
sent to the space testing grounds. They landed at the
spaceport's airport and were met by a limousine that
was especially sent to meet them.

These men were especially chosen by each of
their countries governments because they were the
best spies, or as the rest of the world called them, representatives that these countries had created. Each
of these representatives were thoroughly trained in
the art of survival. That meant that they practiced
self preservation as well as murder if it was called
for. That was their only purpose. They were trained
to protect the motherland no matter what. They
worked alone and had no mates. They were loners.

They had been given portfolios of the other two
representatives because they needed to know who
they were being judged against.

These men were chosen because their governments felt that they were the most loyal representatives that they could offer to open a door into the
outer space industry. They were sure that they would
accomplish the mission that they were assigned to.
None had ever failed a mission before.

They entered the limousine. Each took a position
that made them feel safe.

"I am Max Von Hardt." I am twenty-six years of age. I speak four languages and I have never been hurt or wounded in any way in the line of performing an assignment."

"Cedric Smith, twenty-four years of age. I also speak four languages and I have only failed one assignment and that was to die for my country."

"Francios Marcos. Twenty-five years of age. I speak very little. I never fail and I complete all assignments."

After this brief but informative introduction they began to compare their intelligence of each other.

"I have studied both of your portfolios and I feel that I now know your abilities almost as well as my own. I haven't been assigned to kill either of you so I must assume that we will be working as a team? This assignment as explained to me is dependent upon all of our efforts to gain access for our countries into the space testing grounds. I now ask you to place your trust in my abilities?"

"Well spoken Max. I too have studied both of your portfolios and never having worked with another countries agent before, I have to feel that I had to understand everything about someone that I am going to have to trust as much as I trust myself. I trust that if I put my hand in yours you will put yours in mine."

"Francios, that was a speech that would make a lesser man cry. I too have studied your portfolios.

I think I understand your abilities and your will to survive any assignment. You are both total loners and will do anything to accomplish a successful ending to an assignment. This one is no different. If it comes to acting alone, either of you will do so to survive. I too will act alone if the successful conclusion of the mission calls for it."

"You do seem to make sense of this assignment. I was not so forward with my true feelings. Like I spoke earlier. I don't say much. I now tell you this. You have a reputation as the most feared and respected representative by all of your superiors. You were sent on this assignment because your country felt you were the best that they could send. After meeting you, you are as in life a legend that a person like me should fear. I will back you up and even stand beside you but I will never turn my back to you. For as I said earlier, I too will survive by failing only one assignment. I will only die in the line of duty."

They had met the challenge of becoming a team. Since the introductions were completed the limousine drove them on their way to complete their assignments. The limousine reached the gate to the Space Testing Grounds. The window that separated the representatives from the driver turned to a smoky hazy ebony colored glass. It then turned into a clear high definition television screen. A figure appeared.

"Greetings!"

"You are now about to take a tour of the Space

Testing Grounds. It is my pleasure and privilege to allow you to inspect the facilities of this very important and hopefully world awakening project. The limousine will be your tour guide. Just relax and enjoy the tour. We are proud of our facility here and we like to treat our recruits with as much comfort as we are able. Now, men of your persuasion are not easy to make comfortable, so the doors will be sealed as well as the windows. Please don't feel that you are in any danger. You are invited guests. I am sorry that we couldn't send someone in person to greet you and welcome you to our facility, but you are very dangerous men."

As the figure on the screen said this the gate to the Space Testing Center opened and the limousine entered it . The figure on the screen spoke again.

"Now to your left is the first of our radar tracking stations. It can monitor a space vehicle as far away as Uranus. If you feel that this is impossible, then look to your right where we have assembled a radio transmitter that can send signals as far as we have satellites. We do have a very intricate and successful system of satellites and bases already. We need manned satellites functioning though. To your direct left is the newest space vehicle that we feel is capable of sustaining life in outer space. It is only a satellite though and can only travel so far before it runs out of fuel. This is our main problem at the moment but we have teams of experts all over the world working on the fuel recycling method that will make a vehicle capable of traveling free in outer space. Some of these vehicles are functioning in space now. In fact, the rocket to your left is due to send provisions to one of our manned satellites in about an hour.

Please! Look to your right again. This is the main center of the Testing Ground. It is the main computer center. It contains computers that are linked to all of the world members countries computers. It has been watching your three countries computers until today. Now, you are probably wondering why we have singled out your three countries computers to watch and why the membership of the testing ground was not granted to all countries? Because our system is linked with the space stations and satellites in outer space, they are not capable of understanding our world problems. We had to make sure that we could make a control computer that would be able to control the rest before we allowed all of the earth's computers to be linked with the testing grounds computers. We now feel safe that the Space Testing Grounds computers will understand that human life is our main priority. We had to make sure that all the computers made the continued life of humans a priority. We now welcome your three countries to the Space Testing Ground. We need manned satellites and no one seems to want to volunteer for the job. The computers tell us that men of your persuasion are the perfect candidates. It is time to fulfill your countries assignment for you. Please look to your left. There are three soon to be manned satellites. Make your choice and remember that you are the best of your profession and that your governments felt you deserved to help them gain entrance into the Space Testing Grounds. Thank you for making it a worldwide space testing ground."

The screen again went smoky hazy and then ebony. The door of the limousine opened automatically. The three representatives looked at one another. They then stepped out of the limousine and chose their satellite. They had been given their final assignment.

THE DEVIL'S SON

THE PRIEST KNEELED AT THE bed of Laura Wilkinson and prayed. He had never been asked to exorcise a demon from a person before. She claimed that she was a virgin and that the Devil had visited her one night and raped her. She was about to give birth to a demon, or the son of Satan himself. The town was not sure what to think. Laura was a christian and attended church regularly. She was a good girl and not known to be in the company of men, especially those that were considered unsavory. She was claiming that the Devil raped her, and now she was giving birth to a baby that could only belong to the Devil. The town priest was expected to make sense of it all. All he could do was pray. If this was a son of Satan then what was he supposed to do?

Laura screamed in agony. The baby wanted to be born. Laura was helpless and so was the priest. All he could do was watch and wait. If indeed the baby was the son of the Devil, then what? Should he kill it or let it grow into a person?

He prayed for an answer, but none was coming. The baby was though, and soon the priest would have to make a choice. He would have to deal with a birth where there was no father and there was a woman that claimed to be a virgin that claimed that she had been raped by the Devil. He moved aside so a mid wife could help deliver the baby. Laura screamed so loud that the townspeople gathered around had to cover their ears.

The priest walked over to a corner and covered his eyes while he prayed for an answer to what he was expected to do. What was he supposed to do? He kept praying for answers, but none were coming. He was going to have to do something and he didn't want the responsibility. If indeed the baby was born of Satan, then he would have to either kill it or place it in a place that it could never know who its father was. Either way Laura would be a problem. She believed that she was giving birth to the Devil's son. What would become of her?

The baby was born. It was a boy and looked as normal as any baby born in the world before. The priest examined it from head to toe. It didn't seem to be evil or have horns or a tail. Was Laura insane or did she really get raped by a demon?

The priest went to his church to gather his thoughts. He went up to the pulpit and sank to his knees. He asked God to tell him what to do next. He knelt there for hours. He was not receiving any answers. He then stood up and returned to the hospital. He needed answers. If Laura had given birth to an unholy baby then he needed to know why.

He entered the room where Laura was being kept. She had to be held down with restraints. She didn't want to see her baby or to have anything to do with him. She kept claiming that he was the Devil's son.

The priest asked Laura why she was afraid of her baby. She answered him.

"He is the Devil's son."

She shivered and the priest saw that she was sweating too much.

She screamed. "I gave birth to the Devil's son!"

She then just died without a whimper.

The priest was holding on to her hand. It went limp and cold. Laura died without a reason. All she could do was to keep saying that she spawned the Devil's son.

The priest went to see the baby. It looked like any normal baby that had just been brought into this world. He moved close to the baby and picked it up. He spoke to it.

"Who are you?"

The baby only a few hours old spoke to the priest.

"I am the Devil's son."

LET US HEAR IT FOR
THE CROWD

———————

"LADIES AND GENTLEMAN TONIGHT IS the night that most of you have been waiting your entire lives for. Tonight you will witness the greatest show on earth!" The ringmaster paraded around a circle that was lit up like it was on fire.

The arena was filled to capacity. The crowd was expecting to see the unexpected. They had witnessed many a circus and acts of daring and death defying feats. They had endured week long festivals of music and drugs. They had even witnessed the invasion of earth by the first aliens, but tonight they were expecting to witness a yet unknown and unheard of experience. Generals were in the crowd, clowns, cowboys, and all the known races in the galaxy were in the crowd. Anyone that could afford a ticket was in the crowd. This was the "Greatest Show on Earth" and everyone wanted to be a part of it.

The ringmaster raised his hands above his head and screamed at the crowd.

"Now ladies and gentleman and all the rest of you, we will start the evening off by introducing you to your host and the only man that can bring you "The Greatest Show on Earth," Sampson Greeley."

The crowd went wild and the applause made hearing anything impossible. Sampson was the best known celebrity in modern times by bringing back the big time circus. A circus always brought out the populace and this time it was again "The Greatest Show on Earth."

He approached the center ring and raised his hands above his head and screamed. "Be silent!"

The arena became so still that a gnat couldn't move without its wings being heard. Sampson walked toward the center of the ring and then looked up into the sky. Sampson never let his shows be televised or recorded by any agency. They were one of a kind performances. He was the king of the circus industry. As he approached the center ring the crowd became so silent that you could hear a whisper and everyone would know what had been spoken.

"Friends, fans, the curious, and all the rest of you. I come to you tonight promising to perform the greatest show on earth! Now you all know that that I only bring a show to you that has never been seen before. Well, tonight I bring to you, and you are here aren't you?" The crowd roared their applause. "The Greatest Show on Earth!"

The crowd went crazy. The cheers were so loud that they could be monitored by satellites hovering above the planet. Sampson raised his hands above his head and circled the ring.

"Please! Please! Save some of your applause for the performers."

The crowd became silent again. Sampson moved his hand to his ear and spoke to the crowd.

"Now that I have your attention!"

The crowd exploded with applause.

"Please! As I said earlier I have for you a show that that has never been equalled before, and I mean never before."

The crowd broke into a cheer.

"Now you know my reputation for being modest."

A reaction from the crowd of relaxed chuckles.

"But tonight I am not going to be modest."

A cheer filled the arena again.

"Tonight I will show you my greatest discovery and the greatest discovery of all times."

The crowd went wild with applause as they screamed their pleasure for being allowed to witness Sampson's newest circus.

"You!" Sampson raised his hands in the air and waved them around at the crowd. "You are about to witness the most spectacular and spellbinding show of your short and uninformed lives. I have spared no expense or dared nothing to take any risk that would not allow me to bring this show into this arena."

The crowd roared their acceptance.

Sampson walked around the center ring like a God. He raised his hands above his head and screamed.

"Tonight I will become a part of the crowd. I want to witness this show myself!"

The crowd roared their pleasure as he took a ring side seat and became silent.

A new ringmaster entered the main ring. All of the lights but one went out. It was positioned on the new ringmaster.

"OK, you have been warned that you will witness something never seen before on earth or anywhere else. So be prepared to see what has never been seen before and please control yourselves. Ladies and gentlemen and everyone else, I am proud and privileged to bring you "The Greatest Show on Earth or Anywhere Else.""

The spotlights lit up the center ring.

"I am proud to let the crowd behold "The Time Warps!""

The ringmaster walked to the center of the ring with the spotlight following him. Figures started appearing out of thin air and more spotlights began to come alive. The figures grew from sticklike characters into Giants. They kept growing until they were the size of twenty human beings. They then turned into strands of light and danced about the arena. The spotlights then went out. The strands of light danced about the arena as if they were not supposed to be anywhere else. The crowd went silent. They were not expecting this.

The light strands joined together in the center ring and exploded into a fireworks display that would make any child feel that they had seen heaven.

Then the center ring lit up. A scene from the old west materialized. Then History was rapidly displayed going forward. It suddenly stopped at the present time. All the prominent figures in the history of earth were shown at their peak of life. They then were burned and disappeared. All of the lights went out.

Round spots started growing from the center ring. These spots started to turn into cylinders. Each was a different color. The structures started to join together like tinker toys. Beams of light projected from each and connected with the other spheres. The spheres kept rotating until the whole arena seemed to become a rainbow. A whine was then heard in the air. It made everyone in the crowd uneasy but the sound seemed to sooth the crowd. They sighed and sat back in their seats. The next part of the show was about to begin.

Sampson stood and raised his hands to the crowd. They saw him and realized that they were seeing something new. He sat down and waited for what was next.

The center ring turned into a pipe organ of a sort. The sound was strange and seemed to mystify the crowd. The crowd started feeling the sound. It was capturing them. It was like the crowd was being pulled into the center ring. Then the sound ceased and the center ring was again in a spotlight.

Faces started appearing in the center ring. They were circus people. The figures then turned into a blinding white sphere. It started spinning and then sparks started to fly from it. It was so unreal that none of the crowd could hold back a shriek or a cry.

The sphere started to shrink and threw smaller spheres into all parts of the arena. The crowd was spellbound. The arena went totally dark. Then a checkerboard appeared in the middle of the center ring. The spaces on the checkerboard started rising and lowering making music. They sounded like old organ music that most people relate to a circus. The checkerboard then folded up and disappeared.

Fireworks erupted in the arena and then everything went dark.

A single spotlight came on and the ringmaster stood facing the crowd.

"So, you are still looking for something new."

He hesitated and turned around to stare at everyone in the crowd. He smiled at the crowd.

"You have just witnessed a show of energy as yet

unleashed on this planet. It was totally created by the "Time Warps."

He stared up at the crowd and then spoke so everyone could hear him.

"You might think that what you saw was just some trick. It was energy. Sit back and enjoy what you will experience next. "The Time Warps" are just beginning to astound you."

A group of strands shot straight up from the center ring. They began to wobble back and forth and then bent to touch the floor of the arena, They then exploded into a mass of strands in all three rings. Each strand was a color that exploded into a sparkler. The crowd was mesmerized by this light show. The strands then joined together and became attached to the center ring. The center ring was being showered with a mass of sparkles. The whole arena was a fireworks show. All three rings were connected to the center ring and the arena was ablaze with the colors of the strands.

Then almost unbeknown to the crowd, in the center of the fireworks, stood or floated above the crowd what seemed to human beings as insects. These were "The Time Warps."

All lights went out and only a single spotlight lit up the four figures.

The crowd let out a gasp.

Sampson stood and pleaded for the crowd to remain calm.

"Please allow the show to continue!"

The crowd somehow managed to contain their horror. Still there was a feeling of unrest in the air. Aliens in the past a had at least resembled some sort of a human form. But insects had always made humans feel uneasy.

Sampson spoke to the crowd. "I have brought these performers to you to put on a show, not to scare you."

At this point the crowd began to shuffle around and tried to regain some sort of composure.

Sampson still facing the crowd pleaded his case.

"Now if you will allow these performers to carry on you will witness energy at its best. They have used your energy to produce tonight's show. They used the crowd's energy."

Sampson Greeley walked into the main ring and turned into what he really was. He looked at the crowd and became one of the insect like creatures. He then joined the other four and hovered with them above the center ring.

The crowd started yelling for these creatures to be destroyed. Laser equipped Security guards started shooting at the "The Time Warps."

"The Time Warps" remained calm and decided to leave the arena. The crowd was still screaming for their destruction. They rose to a level where no laser blasts could injure them and communicated in the way of their species.

"I told you that earth was still not ready for our kind. It has always been like that. I remember when the Egyptians thought that we were reptiles. I liked being the apelike creatures for the Tibetans though. The humans do have much to learn. But they did put on a good show for us this time. I think that we all agree. Let us hear it for the crowd."

It Was a Crazy War

ALLEN WALKED OVER TO THE timer and stared at it long and hard. It was just so hard to believe that in just four more hours if no word came from the superiors he could not stop the trigger mechanism that would destroy the whole planet. Allen had been chosen for this assignment because he completed the best broadcast of the earth's farewell message. The superiors asked any and everyone to put on a disk their version of what had happened in just one year on the planet. The war that started only just a year earlier was now totally out of control. The switch that would start the timer that ended earth hummed and then turned on twenty hours ago. Allen had been locked in a secure area that controlled the death switch that unless was turned off would send out satellites broadcasting the end of earth. Allen would be the last person that the superiors could contact to stop the end of the world. If no word came in the next four hours he would be helpless to save the world and would send out warnings of what happened in capsules that described the war. It would be his last broadcast, and in fact the last broadcast from earth. Allen didn't want the earth to end. He had written and produced his disk because he was a student of movies and television and felt he had the knowledge capable of making a very graphic and believable story about the war.

His disk was chosen and because of it he was taken by force by the superiors and given the job of ending the earth and to send out his description of how it ended. He was locked in a room with orders to place his disks and players in capsules that would tell the story of the war and the destruction of earth. He was to send them into outer space and then to destroy the planet unless he was given the order to terminate the destruction by the superiors.

Allen could do nothing but wait. If no call came in from the superiors he would end earth and send satellites into outer space explaining why. He had twenty-four hours to stop the destruction of earth unless the armies declared peace. It would be the last war on earth! He stared at the timer.

Allen was a news broadcaster at a San Francisco television station. He studied what had happened so quickly that no country, race, or person could possibly understand how the world could end in just months. It was a crazy war. It raged out of control in just weeks and became uncontrollable in a month and some days, and then became a global disaster in less than two months. He was now given the nightmare or duty of ending the planet because of a war that went out of control. He was locked in a room because he saw the war in a way that explained it and put it on a disk. It would be a reminder to anyone or anything that came upon the satellites in the future. The war was crazy and it was insane. Allen was now in control and locked in a room that no one could enter unless peace happened.

He sat at a table and waited for his final dinner. He had poisoned the food so that he would die just before the end of the planet took place. He was going to eat steak, potatoes and a salad. He poured himself a glass of red wine and turned on the video screen. He wanted to understand the reason why he was the one chosen to film the end the planet. The screen went white and he saw himself.

"This is Allen Andrews describing the history of the race war. It began when the first two different skinned humans decided that they were no longer compatible. Each wanted to rule the planet. They decided that the other had to be erased. This was an awkward beginning of a war because other races decided that they too should be considered. It was no longer black against white. It was variations of the two and other colored people that made the war turn very ugly fast. Loyalties came and went.

Soon there were no more countries, there was only a planet of races that wanted to destroy the rest. There were no mixed race armies at first, but then as this next group of videos shows, the intelligent humans formed some sort of an alliance. The war seemed to become at a stand still. The mixed race armies general led by Charles Domino Velasques and "Happy" Jack Johnson seemed to out maneuver the one race armies and won several major victories.

The spy system set up by these two generals was so vast that none of the one race armies had any way to remain undetected when they wanted to attack one another. The mixed race army was always there after a battle to take any left over soldiers into their army. Soon they had so many defeated recruits as to make up an army that just wanted to win. The one race armies were forced to form countries once again. This was what should have been the point where peace negotiations could begin but then one of the countries because it was now stationary began plans to launch atomic bombs into outer space above the planet. The spy system fell apart when the one race armies became stationary. The mixed race army had more countries but was the easiest to attack. The one race armies just kept showering the mixed race countries with missiles while building nuclear weapons which they planned to send into outer space above the planet. It then became a crazy war. No one could win the war because each side needed to eradicate the other. The problem was that one side would end the world before it was defeated. With all of the missiles being exploded and other forms of genocide being tried the planet became uninhabitable on the surface. All armies had to go underground.

Now the war was being fought in vehicles that were climate controlled. The surface of the planet was so contaminated that it could not sustain any life.

A leader rose to power in the mixed army. This man, Garland Henry, whose picture is now being shown, sent the first manned satellites into space above the planet to strike the one race's countries with weapons yet unheard of in the history of the world. He was a scientist but he also had a military background.

This should have ended the war but the one race countries countered this maneuver by launching atomic bombs into the atmosphere, exploding them making the whole surface of the planet and the space above it uninhabitable.

That was when the mixed race armies formed the superiors. They were the power on the planet that would decide when to end all life. They sent out a warning and began to collect disks about the war. The winning disk would be allowed to end the planet and send out its message to future explorers if there were any. Allen was the winner, but he didn't feel like he had won anything. He sat at his table with his last meal and stared at the countdown clock. Allen was just an instrument that could cause the destruction of the planet. He started eating his meal. There was only fifteen minutes before the superiors could call off the end of the planet. He ate a piece of steak and sipped some wine. Allen collapsed on the floor. He died of a heart attack. There were still eleven minutes on the timer. The timer turned on ten minutes before the end of the planet would take place. Allen's disks would be sent into outer space. The world would end.

A Game of Chance

"MISS PERRIWEATHER SEND HARP IN when he shows up. He is back on the active agent's roster and I need him for an assignment."

"Will do boss. I'll send him in just as soon as he shows up."

Harp leans over the desk and kisses his finger and touches Miss Perriweather's lips.

"Harp! You are back?"Miss Perriweather swoons. She is in love with Harp.

"The one and only. So, did everyone miss me?"

"I will admit that it has been dull around here since you went into rehab. The boss hasn't had a reason to scream or yell profanities to anyone in particular for almost two months. That is the exact amount of time you have been in rehab."

"Well!" Harp twirled in a circle. "What do you think? Am I as good as new?"

"You look as fresh as the day you entered this office as the newest recruit to be picked by the IIA."

Harp laughed. He was a gangly 25 year old when he applied for the IIA. He had never held a job for more than a year or two and those years were usually filled with his being put on probation or suspension for various acts that were not conducive to business. He barely graduated from a junior college, yet he was still determined fit to carry a weapon and join the most powerful law enforcement agency in the universe. He somehow managed to be recruited and graduate from the IIA training school. He lived through three years with the agency and today was officially declared finished with rehabilitation from the right side of his body being crushed by a mutant robot on his last assignment. He was now reactivated as an agent for the Intergalactic Intelligence Agency. Harp was ready to live and die if necessary to keep the galaxy safe again.

He had performed 6 missions for the agency and completed them all without being killed or disfigured to the point that he could not be rebuilt. Most agents would be promoted and given a coush position in the agency after 6 missions, but Harp was just too unpredictable and uncontrollable. He was listed by the agency as good for only one thing, suicide missions.

The boss was getting impatient. He buzzed Miss Perriweather again.

"Where is Harp?"

She looked at Harp. He smiled, then turned his head sideways, stuck out his tongue and opened the door to the bosses office. He pretended to still be the wounded agent that was rebuilt after being crushed by a mutant robot on his last mission, which he still managed to finish successfully. The boss, known only as HMS, stared at Harp and tried to gain control of the meeting. He then punched his intercom button. "Miss Perriweather, send in Sanders."

His voice displayed the fire and irritation in it that Harp always seemed to bring out of him.

He spoke to Harp harshly.

"I know that you just finished a long rehabilitation process but this next mission cannot be given to an agent who is not fit and ready. So if you are not ready for an assignment, tell me now!"

Sanders entered the office and leaped at Harp. He sidestepped the advance and chopped Sanders on his neck rendering him helpless in less than a minute. Harp stood above Sanders in case he might want to try something else, but he held up his hand in surrender.

Harp turned to HMS and said, "Are you satisfied?"

HMS tells Sanders to leave while Harp goes over to the drug cabinet and pours himself a blueberry stabilizer. He turns to HMS and says, "Want to join me?"

HMS waves him off.

"We are going to bypass the normal procedures on this next assignment. You will only report to and get your orders directly from me. No one else will know who you are and cannot give you any aid. You will be injected with a tracking devise that so far no one including ourselves can detect in an agent unless it is activated. You will need to activate it only if you are too damaged to finish the assignment or if you have completed it. You must push your eyebrows together. No one would suspect this from you. Do you understand that this is a suicide mission?"

Harp put his thumb up, a sign that meant all was well in any dialect.

"As of today your existence in the galaxy will be erased and you will be given a new identity. You will be welcome among the law abiding establishments in the galaxy and some of the illegal ones. You will be known as Louis Darryl Harp, a playboy that inherited his wealth. We decided to give you a name you could easily remember. You will have unlimited credits at your disposal anywhere in the galaxy. This does not mean that you can take our credits and run. They will be monitored as you access them. This is just a way to help you keep your cover as a playboy. Just play the part."

Justin Wells enters HMS's office. He is the head of research and development. He looks at Harp and shakes his head. Harp walks over to the drug cabinet and pours another stabilizer only this time doubles the dose. Wells speaks to HMS.

"Does he even know how dangerous this assignment is?"

"Harp is a secret agent. He just finishes what we ask him to. What gadgets have you prepared for him?"

Harp gulps down his double stabilizer and walks over to Wells. They have met before and Harp has been thankful for his gadgets. They saved his ass several times. He walks back to the drug cabinet and pours himself a triple dose this time. Wells always has devices that make Harp fear where he is headed. If Wells shows up then Harp knows he is going to enter Hell or worse. So far Wells has given him some tools that have gotten him back to headquarters and into rehab. He gulps the stabilizer and walks over to Wells.

"So what special aids do you have for me this time?"

"This is a portable force field. It does have one slight drawback. It takes three-seconds to become functional. It lasts for ten minutes though on each charge and is inpenatratable as far as we have tested it. It has six discharges and is worn as a belt. It is quite heavy and can only be activated by you, that is if you are wearing it? You must press your finger on this screen to activate each discharge. Never let someone else take it from you or it will become inoperable for a day if someone other than you tries to activate it after being removed from your body. Do you understand this?"

Harp picked up the belt.

"It is heavy. I may need some more rehabilitation if I am going to have to wear this."

"The weight is unavoidable but it is an incredible safety devise. Ok, now we have what I am calling "The Well's Crank." It is a weapon like none other in the galaxy. It looks like your conventional stun gun but it is much more. It speeds up the victims metabolism at such a fast rate as to make the victim black out in less than half the time a conventional stun gun would take. It can also be reversed to act as a stimulant to counter any stunning agents that you encounter. It only has two settings, one for victim, two for stimulant. It is very simple to use and is lighter than any weapon that is in use at this point in time."

"It is very nice and I can slip it under my force field belt."

"These are not toys and you need to take them as serious life saving devises. We have made these devises because you will be in constant danger and our department has taken on the job of making it easier for you to survive missions."

Harp put on the belt and tucks the Well's Crank in the right side of it. He is left handed and can draw it out faster. He draws it and points it at HMS.

"So, what is the assignment?"

Harp points to Wells.

"Get out of here unless you have more life saving gadgets for me. I have an assignment."

Wells walks out and shoots the finger at Harp.

"You don't deserve our technology and I still have to code the weapons to your DNA."

Harp screams at him.

"I'll only thank you if I see you again!"

"Harp you are the most..." The door slams and cuts off Well's response.

Miss Perriweather laughs out loud and says under her breath. "Now that is how this office should sound."

Wells runs for the safety of the research labs.

Harp walks over to the drug cabinet but HMS stops him. He turns and stares at HMS.

"So this time it is serious?"

"Illegal gambling is rampant and we need to control it. There is a man by the name of George Sage who is the enforcer for a woman by the name of Gloria Goldmine. She owns the illegal casino known to us as Sandy Beach as well as many legal gambling casinos in the galaxy. She has also been rumored to be trying to take over all of the other illegal gambling off planet casinos. She has avoided all galaxy law enforcement agencies. George Sage has been linked to many murders and seems to think that he can kill anyone in the galaxy at will to protect the illegal gambling on off planet sites. Gloria Goldmine and George Sage must be taken down or destroyed. You must either kill them or they will kill you. You do not exist in the real world anymore accept as your new identity. You are a very special secret agent. I am the only person that can make you a part of the galaxy again, that is if you complete this assignment. Don't fail or your last rehabilitation will seem like a resort visit. Gloria Goldmine and George Sage want to rule the galaxy and will if they succeed in taking over all illegal gambling in the universe. You must stop them. Your assignment is to stop or kill them. You must not fail!"

Harp understood his mission. He walked out of HMS's office and didn't even wink at Miss Perriweather. She knew this must be a very dangerous assignment. Harp was taking it serious. She tried to smile as HMS boomed on the intercom.

"Miss Perriweather, Set up a meeting with all of the galaxies head of states."

Harp was now all alone in the galaxy. Miss Perriweather wondered if he would ever enter HMS's office again. She watched as Harp left the office. He just smiled. She shivered. Harp turned and shoved his thumb up. He had just been given unlimited credits in all parts of the universe and a license to kill. He felt alive again. No one lives forever unless they beat the game. Harp was ready to play to win. He had an assignment and he hoped his opponents were worthy of him. He would risk his life once again for the IIA. He was playing the ultimate game of chance.

Harp had twenty minutes until his transport took off for Gama. Gama was the most popular gambling planet in the galaxy. It had no other use. All natural resources had been mined from it long ago. It now only existed for prostitution, gambling, and producing cheap labor. Those that lost all their worldly possessions could be bought cheap and sent to planets that needed cheap laborers. It had a strong IIA security force that maintained the safety of visitors. Harp entered the transport and ordered two stabilizers laced with lotus blossoms. These were supposed to make a person feel euphoric while transporting between planets. Harp was not sure where he was heading but he wanted to be euphoric. Harp was seated in the front of the transport where only the most wealthy travelers paid to be seated. He patted the stewardess on her butt and said, " I will gamble on you if you are game?"

She turned toward him and looked deep into his eyes. She seemed to like his advances.

"My name is Brenda."

"I am Louis Darryl Harp. I am a gambler and now I guess a fool. You just touched my heart with your stare and I owe you an apology."

"I liked it. You just touched my best body part. If you want to try and touch the rest of me then keep ordering stabilizers and ask for me. I also have a layover on Gama and wouldn't mind showing you around."

"Brenda!" he whispered her name and then exhaled.

Harp was intoxicated with her scent. He drained the two stabilizers as if they were water. They were making him euphoric or was it Brenda who was making him feel so? He pushed the button that would bring a stewardess to his seat. Brenda showed up.

He reached over and patted her butt again.

"You wicked man!"

He grabbed her ass.

"Now you will have to buy me dinner,"

Harp was amazed. Nothing came this easy, especially not a woman.

"I am now really confused. Who are you?"

"I have a long rest stop on Gama. I could show you around if you want?"

Harp was mesmerized by Brenda. He was on an assignment. He couldn't be side tracked by a beautiful woman? He just didn't know what or where he was headed and Brenda seemed to be a good start on Gama. He spoke to her.

"Bring me two more stabilizers with lotus blossoms and I will take you up on your offer to show me around Gama."

She looked deep into his eyes. "You will not regret this."

He caved into his desires. Brenda was what he

wanted right now. Harp was now just a man who was lusting for a woman and he had all the credits in the galaxy at his disposal. He shook his head. He was on an assignment. Brenda's scent was making him feel like a schoolboy in love. He had to regain his focus. He was hoping Brenda would join him on Gama.

The transport landed on Gama and Harp collected his luggage and waited to see if Brenda would really show up. She walked out of the spaceport and into his arms. He was mesmerized by her. She spoke.

"Let's go to my place first."

Harp kissed her like he wanted to inhale her. Brenda kissed back as if she wanted to be inhaled. Harp waved for a robocab. He would go wherever Brenda wanted him to go. He was intoxicated by her. He was on an assignment but it somehow was not so important anymore. Brenda had him thinking that he was just a man. He said to the driver. "Go where ever she says."

They ended up at a very nice complex near the casinos on Gama. Brenda was no tramp. She was living large and Harp paid the taxi driver and carried his bags into the lift that would take them to Brenda's living space. The door opened to a spacious room that looked out upon the planet. Brenda was not just a stewardess on a transport. Harp asked her, "Who are you?"

"I am Brenda Sage. My father is a very powerful man on this planet and in the galaxy. He takes care of things. I have had to take jobs that are not in the limelight so I could live free of his watchful eye. I have always wanted to be a free soul but he has made me a prisoner because he is so important. I just want to find a man like you and run away. Can you take me away to somewhere in space that no one knows about George Sage?"

Harp shook his head. Sage? He was looking for a man by the name of George Sage. Could he have found the one person that would allow him to meet the man? He hoped not. He liked Brenda. She pulled him down on a sofa. They made love several times. Harp then asked her, "Should I unpack?"

Harp awoke next to Brenda. They made love, he didn't know how many times. She smelled so sweet he wanted to suck on her. He flashed his memories and came upon the memory of her saying she was Brenda Sage. He was on an assignment that he might have to kill Gloria Goldmine and her enforcer George Sage. Brenda seemed too easy a way for him to gain access to these people. He looked at her and became confused. He was an IIA agent on a mission. Brenda was on his transport to Gama. Was his assignment compromised and did they know he was coming? Was he being set up? At the moment all he wanted to do was lick Brenda from her toes to her head. He was intoxicated by a woman.

Brenda stared into Harp's eyes. "I want to show you a planet of games of chance."

"I was born a gambler and you could just be my lady luck."

"If you can take me away from this planet and my father then I am yours."

Harp kissed her and she inhaled his heart. He was now on two assignments. Brenda was his ticket out of the IIA and he knew that he would have to kill her father to accomplish both missions. Killing George Sage and Gloria Goldmine was not going to be easy though. They were very connected and he had just come to a dump planet. He would have to use Brenda to enter the illegal casinos. He licked her belly and tried not to fall in love. She tasted like lotus blossoms. He knew he could never give her up. He would kill her father and his employer and then try to take her away to a place that she would never have to think about her father again. She smelled like lotus blossoms. He made love to her again. He vowed under his breath to kill her father and set her free.

Brenda came to Harp after showering dressed in a white evening dress. She had ordered a black tuxedo for Harp. He showered and the tuxedo was delivered. He dressed and they looked liked the perfect couple. They left her living space and entered a robocab headed for the casino district. She was going to show Harp Gama. It was her home planet. She just didn't know that Harp was a secret agent and was wearing a force field belt and carrying a Well's crank pistol. He was on an assignment. He was in love with Brenda but he still had a job to finish. Gloria Goldmine and George Sage were his targets and he needed a way to find them on Gama. He would use Brenda, if need be, to find them. They entered one of the most exclusive casinos on Gama. All eyes were on them as they entered. Harp's eyes were on everyone else. He knew he was either being set up or he was going to get closer to his targets. He was not sure which.

Harp's ID was scanned and he and Brenda were given a badge when they entered the casino. They were priority one. That meant they had no limit when it came to betting. Brenda kissed him deeply. "Let's gamble."

Harp felt Brenda's body next to his. He wanted to save her. Harp looked around. He couldn't tell if he was being set up. Brenda was just a beautiful woman on his arm. He did a 360 degree view of the casino and didn't see anything that seemed like a threat. He relaxed and led Brenda to a roulette table. She bet 1000 credits on red. Harp placed another 500 on 00. The ball jumped several times as the wheel spun and landed in 00.

Brenda squealed as Harp collected his winnings.

He then placed four 500 credit chips on 5, 19, 29, and 32. Brenda placed another 1000 on Black. The wheel spun and the little white ball kept jumping before landing in 29 black. Brenda started jumping up and down. Harp watched the crowd as Brenda collected their winnings. Harp wanted to be noticed and he was sure that he was making that happen. He hugged Brenda and yelled out loud, "What can I do to make you happy?" He kissed her deeply.

"I bet 10,000 on red. Lady luck is on my side." Brenda kisses him and then yells, "This is the man!"

The ball falls into 11 red. Everyone around the table applauds and Harp collects his winnings and heads for a table near a bar. Harp scans the casino. A winner is always a mark for someone and he wants to know who will come after him. He hopes it is an illegal casino person. Winnings are taxed on the gambling planets but not on the illegal casinos. Harp is being taxed at 20%. He just made the galaxy several thousand credits. He is ahead but he still had to pay. He waits at his table and orders a stabilizer with lime. Brenda orders a tranquilizer fizz. He drains his stabilizer and orders two more. He feels lucky and because they are a very attractive couple he wants to keep everyone's eyes on them.

He leads Brenda to a black jack table. The waitress delivers his two stabilizers and he gives her a 100 credit tip. Brenda kisses him and he bets 1000 on two spots. Brenda bets a 500 credit chip on a third spot. Harp kisses Brenda and yells, "This is for my lady luck!"

He draws a jack and a king and a ten and deuce. Brenda draws a five and a six. The dealer has a five showing. Harp holds on both hands. Brenda draws a king. The dealer takes a card, a nine of diamonds. He busts. Brenda kisses Harp so hard he thinks he might just be in love. He now has everyone looking at them. He is hoping that he will be approached by someone who can get him on a transport to an illegal casino. He leads Brenda to a table near the bar. Brenda is clouding his mind though. He really likes her. If she is George Sage's daughter then what will she think of him after he kills her father?

He is on an assignment and has a license to kill. He kills people and he is good at his job. George Sage will be just another notch on his gun. Brenda was never supposed to happen to him. He wasn't supposed to be a man. He is a secret agent with a license to kill. He shakes his head and looks around.

A couple comes over to Harp's table.

"Mr Harp! I am Desmond Thames and this is Rachel Jacobs. We could not help but notice your remarkable luck and wondered if you would like to join us for some gambling at a more relaxing spot?"

Harp looked them over and knew at once that they were somebodies. They were too perfect. They had been cosmetically engineered. They belonged to some corporation or were just very rich and powerful people. He invited them to join him. He introduced himself and Brenda.

They joined them. Then Desmond spoke to Harp in a whispered voice. "I know who Brenda is. She is

George Sage's daughter. You are not just gambling on Gama anymore. We need to find out who you are."

Harp raised his hand for a waitress to come to the table." I will have a lotus blossom stabilizer and give the rest of the table what they desire."

He looked into Desmond's eyes. He could not decide what he was seeing. He just kept staring. Desmond responded with a look that Harp didn't expect. He too was a killer. Harp spoke to Rachel.

"You are so lovely. How did you two meet?"

Rachel was chiseled to the point of being too perfect. She had the smell of some sort of intoxicating lotions. Harp was almost getting high on her scent. He looked at Brenda to bring him back to reality. Brenda was so lovely that he almost forgot that he was on an assignment. He looked back at Rachel. "So, how did you two meet?"

"It is a boring story. We do enjoy gambling though and would welcome some company. Please accept our invitation to gamble at some very different spots."

Brenda took Harp's hand and squeezed it hard. "Oh! Please let's gamble some more."

Harp looked at Desmond and Rachel. "Lead us to the next casino but first tell me about Brenda's father?"

"In time Mr. Harp! In time! You said you came to gamble, so let us move on to where the real chances lie."

Harp paid the waitress and they left the casino in a robocab. Brenda held onto Harp as if she would never let him go. He watched as Desmond and Rachel entered the cab. They were too cool. He didn't trust them but knew they would do nothing that might hurt Brenda. Harp had that on his side. He found out that they were headed for the most exclusive casino on Gama. You could not enter it unless you were known on Gama. Obviously Desmond and Rachel fit the bill. Harp took Brenda's hand and followed Desmond and Rachel into "The Waterfall Casino" the most exclusive casino on Gama. Harp was prepared to pay the one million credit entry fee for himself and Brenda but Desmond motioned for him to forget it. "I own this establishment. Your credit is good here. I did a very extensive background check on you. You are wealthy and seem to be a player. George Sage does not share my view of you though. Please gamble. Rachel and I will leave you two lovebirds to your future. Please don't thank us. We just follow orders."

Harp felt down and grabbed his Well's Crank. The pistol and forcefield belt now seemed like necessities. He asked Desmond again.

"Tell me about Brenda's father?"

"That Mr. Harp is for Brenda to tell you if she decides to do so."

He watched as Desmond and Rachel walk away. They had done their job. He was Brenda's new boyfriend. He was now noticed though and George Sage was not a man that you took lightly. Brenda was now his only key to entry into illegal gambling. He just hoped he would not cause her death in the quest.

Harp felt naked. Desmond and Rachel just left him in the middle of a world he could not even try to control. Brenda was clouding his mind and he wasn't thinking like a secret agent that had an assignment to finish. He now understood that he had been drugged at the last casino. He tried to vomit up the drug that he had been given but he passed out.

Harp awoke next to Brenda. She had been drugged also. He was naked and his forcefield belt and Well's Crank were nowhere near him. Brenda was naked. He shook her and she awoke confused and in a bad mood. She yelled. "What the fuck is happening!"

"You tell me. Your father is George Sage."

They were in a king sized bed in a very nice hotel room. The sheets were satin and Harp seemed to slip on them. He grabbed Brenda and held her close to him.

"Why are we here?"

"I didn't tell you about my father because he controls my coming and goings. I thought that maybe you were my escape from his grasp. I know that Rachel and Desmond are under his control. I have never been free to just be me and my father needs to control everything, including my life. I want it to end. Can you save me Harp?"

Harp hugged Brenda so hard he thought he might hurt her. "I will take you away from your father's grasp. I promise you!"

She kissed him so deeply that he thought he would suffocate. He made love to her several times. Brenda stared into his eyes and spoke. "I don't think that I ever want to be separated from you again."

Harp was now lost. He was a secret agent on an assignment to kill her father and Gloria Goldmine but he was in love. He knew that they were probably being monitored on some sort of video equipment so he made love to her again. He thought that if George Sage was watching he might as well make him see his daughter enjoy life for a change. He collapsed after climaxing and Brenda curled up next to him. "You are now my world."

Harp licked his lips. George Sage would now have to invite him into his world. Harp was still a secret agent. Brenda might be the love of his life but finishing an assignment was always a priority. He kissed Brenda.

"I am starved. Let's go to dinner."

Harp got out of bed and moved over and opened a closet. There were clothes in it for formal dining. He checked the closet. His Well's Crank and force-field belt were not there. He acted like it was no big deal. He spoke to Brenda.

"I think someone is expecting us for dinner."

Harp and Brenda showered and dressed in the

clothes that were in the closet. They walked over to the hotel door and it opened as they neared it. They were expected. They entered a hallway that had only one exit. It was a lift to where they could only guess.

Harp looked at Brenda and whispered into her ear. "When were you going to tell me that we would become prisoners here on Gama?"

She turned to him. "Now you know how powerful my father is?"

"I am here to kill him and Gloria Goldmine. I am a secret agent. So, if you really want to be free from your father, I am the man to accomplish the job. If you are not ready to leave your past then let them kill me. I have fallen in love with you and would rather die right now then not tell you the truth. Can you let me do my job?"

Brenda kissed him. "Just get it done. I don't want to live the way I have had to any longer. My father is a bad man and Gloria Goldmine is worse. The galaxy is better off without them, so do your job."

Harp squeezed her hand as the lift opened. He was still on an assignment and now Brenda was with him. He kissed her and whispered. "I don't have any weapons. They took them. Do you know how I can get them back?"

She looked at Harp. "I will tell them to return your weapons. I will tell him they will only be used to protect me. My father is a bad man but he understands that I need to be protected. Just don't act like he is not able to protect me. He sees me as a child. I am a woman, your woman. Protect me and take me away from my father and this planet. Promise me that you will take me away from this Hell. I just want to be free."

The door opened and Desmond and Rachel stared at them. Harp and Brenda exited the lift. The doors closed behind them. Harp held out his hand.

"I am Louis Daryl Harp, I hope you approve of my keeping company with Brenda. If not just kill me where I stand as I am helpless."

Desmond belted out a loud laugh. "You make me laugh. I like that in a man."

Desmond and Rachel had enough information about Harp to let him continue to be Brenda's escort. They also monitored their love making. Desmond spoke to Rachel.

"He seems to have a way of pleasing her. Does he meet your approval?"

Rachel nods. "Brenda is an adult and sex is just normal. As long as he doesn't cause a problem with our business then I have no problem with him."

"Let us go to dinner then. I want to get to know this man that you seem to like so much."

They walk into the most exclusive restaurant on Gama.

Harp was now very sure that he and Brenda would be headed for an illegal casino. He just had to make Desmond and Rachel take an interest in him.

He knew that George Sage would never trust him totally. He held onto Brenda's arm and spoke to Desmond and Rachel.

"I will pick up the check, that is if it won't offend either of you?"

Desmond bellowed out another loud laugh.

"I just might get to like you. Rachel and I own this establishment. There will be no check."

Harp smiles and turns to Brenda. "I think I can get to like these two."

He would have to find a way to get closer to them though or he might just die before finishing his assignment. There were three body protectors following them, two in front and who knew how many cameras and other protectors that were watching them. He just held Brenda's arm and let what would happen take place. Brenda then walked up to Desmond's side.

"Give Daryl back his weapons. He needs them to feel that he can protect me."

He looked her in the eyes. He studied her stare. "You really like this man?"

"Yes, I do. He is the best man that I have ever met and he makes me happy."

At this opportunity Harp moved up and spoke to Rachel. "You are very beautiful and I can tell a powerful woman when I smell her. I am just a rich playboy that has hopefully met his match with Brenda. I admit that I carry weapons and gamble, but then a man has to protect himself as well as indulge in a few vices. I like to gamble and can afford to. I just like the thrill of betting against the odds. I love a good game of chance."

Rachel turned toward him and looked him over. She then spoke.

"You just might get more than you bargained for by making George Sage take an interest in you."

"I was hoping I would also get you to notice me?"

She looked him over again. "You are either very brave or a fool?"

"I am just a modest and not a very intelligent gambler."

He inhaled and spoke.

"Oh I am sorry that was my older brother that died on a slave planet and was eaten by rats and crows."

Rachel chuckled. "You do amuse me. I think I will keep my eyes on you."

Harp backed off. He made his introduction. He just hoped it was good enough to get him into an illegal gambling casino. Brenda joined him as Desmond and Rachel moved side by side and backed behind Harp and Brenda. Rachel spoke to Desmond.

"Keep a close eye on this Harp." She looked at Desmond.

"Give him back his weapons but make sure when he has them we are in a buffered environment. He seems too cool somehow, but he and Brenda do make a handsome couple."

Desmond looks at them. He thinks that Brenda is in love with the guy. He had his men study the weapons, but they could not get them to work. This made him suspicious. The four of them ate dinner.

After dinner they excused themselves.

Brenda handed Harp the key to a suite in the most exclusive hotel on Gama.

"They have given you permission to woo me!"

Harp kissed her. He wasn't happy with this assignment because he was going to have to probably kill Brenda's father and Gloria Goldmine and destroy their off planet gambling enterprises. Still Brenda was tasting very sweet when he kissed her. They moved to the lifts that would take them to their new suite. Harp was infatuated with Brenda. Her father and Gloria Goldmine were becoming blurs to him. Brenda was making him careless and that was not expected from an agent of IIA.

Brenda and Harp entered the suite and found a bottle of champaign that had a note attached to it.

"Enjoy your night."

Harp popped the cork. Champaign was illegal, but on Gama that did not seem to matter. He just wanted to make love to Brenda. He poured two glasses of the illegal juice and noticed that it had a strange odor. He noticed the Well's Crank and force field belt were laying on a chair in the room. He took the Well's Crank and placed it on two. He injected a full potion. He and Brenda then drank the special drink that had been prepared for them. They passed out immediately. They were drugged and ready for transporting to Sandy Beach.

Harp awoke on a transport next to Brenda. There were many other passengers on the transport. He looked around. Everyone was in a deep sleep. His injection of the Well's Crank made him the only one awake. He stood up and walked around the transport. No one was going to wake up soon. He slapped a few people just to make sure. They were drugged. He walked the whole passenger seating area. There was no stewardess or any guards. He was the only functioning human on the transport except for the pilots. He took his seat next to Brenda and played like he was comatose. He was not sure that his cover was blown but he was sure that George Sage knew he was coming. He was about to gain his access to Sandy Beach but at what price? He lay back in the comfortable seat and tried to imagine Brenda's lips kissing him.

The transport stopped and most of the passengers began to awaken. Harp pretended that he too was just awakening. Brenda asked him where they were?

"I really am not sure."

He hugged his belt and felt around for his Well's Crank. He had both of them but wasn't sure if they had been tampered with. He walked with Brenda into Sandy Beach, the most notorious illegal casino in the galaxy. He was not sure if he would make it to the casino floor because he had been drugged and transported without any support from the IIA. He was all alone but he had weapons. He would use them. He was on an assignment. He smiled at George Sage and Gloria Goldmine.

"Welcome to Sandy Beach!"

Harp smiled but noticed that the welcoming committee was not looking at him and Brenda. They were looking at armed guards. Brenda grabbed his hand and squeezed it hard. Harp and Brenda allowed most of the other passengers to exit the transport before they exited. Brenda let out a gasp!

"That is my father!"

Harp put his arm around Brenda and led her up the ramp to Sandy Beach and into the presence of George Sage.

"So, you must be George Sage, Brenda's father?"

"I see that Brenda has confided in you. You must be an extraordinary man because Brenda has never told any of her marks about our relationship."

"Brenda is an unpredictable woman."

"I think that I don't have all the information about you that I would like Mr. Harp. Your weapons are unlike any that I have ever encountered before. You may not keep them while visiting Sandy beach.

You must understand that we are the ones that provide the protection here."

"These weapons were made especially for me and I am a man that likes to possess something that needs an explanation."

"I won't underestimate you then Mr. Harp for I am a man that expects explanations."

"Father, I am only acting as Mr. Harps guide."

"Don't try to deceive me Brenda. I have had you both under surveillance since you docked on Gama. I even took the precaution of listening to your pillow talks. I have many questions about Mr. Harp that need to be addressed before I allow him access to Sandy Beach."

"Brenda is only here because I told her that I would take her with me when I leave."

"Not so Mr. Harp, Brenda is working for me. She brings me marks and she will continue working for me until I say different."

"You and your business! I am nothing more to you than entertainment for your marks. I hate you!"

George Sage has two of his guards grab Brenda and drag her away from Harp.

"Brenda, you must not make a scene here. Tranquillize her and take her to the awaiting transport. Her business is finished here. But you, Mr. Harp, have found yourself in a very dangerous situation. You can either be a guest or a prisoner. It will all depend upon what you decide to do next."

Harp decides to not be either. He pushes the first discharge on his belt. He smiles at George Sage as he awaits for it to materialize.

"I will not gamble without Brenda."

"Brenda may or may not join you. You will now join me for an interview."

"Not on my schedule."

Harp was now enclosed in a forcefield.

He charges George Sage and his mercenaries.

Harp knows his time will either end or begin now. Brenda has been taken from him. He is in a forcefield and wants to end George Sage's rule. He charges ahead not caring if he kills everyone.

He crushes several guards against walls and watches them fall. George Sage escapes by using his guards as his escape plan. Harp could kill many more of George Sage's guard but he still would escape. He kills his guards by crushing them against walls. George looks hard and long at Harp. He wants to kill him. He was not welcome on Sandy Beach. Brenda may love him but he was not a welcome guest here.

"Kill him!"

George Sage retreats.

Harp keeps crushing people against walls. He is on an assignment. Wells would be proud of his belt.

Harp kills as many guards as he can face in 10 minutes.

He still didn't have a clear sight on George Sage.

His force field evaporated and he falls helpless to a floor that is littered with dead bodies of Sandy Beaches security guards. He is now a person that would be killed upon sight. He looks around. Death is everywhere. He has killed many of George Sage's guards. He has failed to kill the only man that matters. He stands up and moves toward a hallway that George Sage retreated into. He is going after him. He is going go kill him. He is the only person that can stop him from loving Brenda. He took her from him and acted like it was just business. Harp wasn't going to do business with George Sage. He was going go kill him. He was on an assignment to kill him and that assignment just became his priority. He was going after George Sage.

He pushes his second discharge. He is sprawled among the dead but is not going to join them if he can help it. He feels the blasts from stun guns. They blacken his vision. He takes over a hundred blasts. George Sage wants him dead. He proceeds down the hallway. He crushes everyone that tries to stop his progress. He is going after George Sage. He has killed all and anyone that is in the hallway. He is on an assignment. He wants to kill George Sage.

He can't see a thing as the stun blasts blackened his force field. He just keeps moving down the hallway absorbing the blasts from behind and ahead. He is chasing George Sage. He has to catch him before he gets to the control room. He takes so many blasts from stun guns that the forcefield is knocked back-wards but it holds. Harp can see nothing. The force field is so blackened by blasts that it is hard for him to move, but he keeps moving forward. He bounces off walls and keeps moving forward. George Sage must die.

He is just about to lose his protection. The force field evaporates and Harp hits the ground hard. He rolls toward the entry and into another hall. He guesses it is going to lead him to the control center of Sandy Beach. He pushes his third discharge. George Sage is going to die and he will kill him.

He sees Gloria Goldmine in front of him. She speaks to him.

"Surrender or die! You cannot leave here alive and Brenda is my prisoner. You are a fool and will die that way."

Harp stands up protected by his third force field.

"You will die and I will make Sandy Beach a memory."

Gloria looks at Harp and then turns and walks away.

"Kill him and send his ashes into space."

George Sage stands in front of Harp and smiles.

"You will die today. My daughter will continue to fill my casinos with marks. You are nothing. I will piss on your grave if there is one."

Harp moves fast and crashes into George.

"You just made the worst mistake in your life. I am here to kill you. Let us begin."

George Sage falls backwards and becomes vulnerable. Harp misses with his crushing blow. George Sage stands up and yells.

"Kill him!"

He is removed by his security guards and Harp is shot at with everything that is available.

Harp holds his breath as he is hit with everything in George Sage's inventory. Blasts of such force would destroy almost anything. Wells force field holds. Harp can see nothing but is sure that he is still alive. He stands up and sees nothing but black. He has survived. He will still kill George Sage. He bounces forward.

George Sage retreats. He is now afraid of Harp. He entered Sandy Beach and told him he was going to kill him. Brenda was his price tag, but he couldn't give her to him. He was the enforcer and would kill anyone who tried to stop Sandy Beach from continuing. Harp was now going to die.

George Sage's reputation was now on the line. Harp had crossed the line between living and dying. George Sage had to kill Harp. There was no other solution.

Harp just kept moving forward. He could see nothing but knew that he was going in the right direction. George Sage would go to the control room of Sandy Beach. Harp would follow him. The end was near. Harp would kill George Sage or die trying. Harp had never died before finishing an assignment. George Sage didn't have that favor on his side. He was an enforcer, he was never supposed to die. Harp kept moving forward. The force field disintegrated and Harp crashed into a wall. He was still alive. He was going to kill George Sage. He pushed his next discharge. He was sure that he was close to the control room and George Sage. He would finish this assignment. He now hated George Sage. He was determined to get Brenda free from his control. He stood up and bounced off walls toward what he hoped was the control center of Sandy Beach.

Harp moved forward. He was going to finish this assignment and would kill George Sage. He actually looked forward to ending George Sage's life. He had taken Brenda away from him without even a blink. He was a killer of men and deserved to die. Harp was just the person to complete the mission. Harp had never been in love before. Brenda awakened a spark in his life that was missing for too many years. He hoped she would forgive him for killing so many people. He knew that they deserved to die but he was being used by a government agency as a killer. He would kill her father and then ask for her forgiveness. He was going to retire from killing. He just had to kill George Sage before he could justify his retirement. Brenda needed to be free from her father. Harp had to kill George Sage.

Harp bounced down the hallway not knowing if he was going in the right direction toward Sandy Beaches control room. He was hit with many blasts from stun guns. He fell backwards but continued his forward motion. He crushed several guards against the walls that were leading him toward the control room.

He moved forward not caring what he would find ahead of him. He had to kill George Sage. That was his only goal. Gloria Goldmine and Brenda would have to be handled next.

George Sage was a monster and he had to kill it. He bounced his way toward the control center and George Sage.

Harp feels for the Well's crank. He had lost it somewhere during his chase. He was defenseless except for the force field. He had used four of them. He was close to the control room. All of a sudden he took blasts from ahead of him. He held his ground but was pushed backwards by the blasts. He wasn't welcome and everything that was available was being used to keep him from reaching the control room. Harp kept moving forward absorbing each blast from the guards. He crashed into the control room and began crushing the guards and all the equipment that controlled the illegal casino. He was not in control though. He was just bouncing off any and everything in the control room. The force field evaporates and Harp was thrown among the instruments and dead bodies. He received many injuries and landed in a pile of dead bodies at the door to the control center. Harp looked up and saw George Sage holding the Wells Crank and pointing it at him.

"Mr. Harp, you are making my life miserable. I think you must die now."

Harp smiled.

"You cannot kill me. I have beaten you. You hold a gun that cannot kill me. I have beaten you. Give up."

George Sage pulled the trigger. Nothing happened. He turned and ran down the hallway.

"You still haven't won."

George Sage was running for the last transport off of Sandy Beach. He didn't want Harp to join him.

George Sage entered the transport.

Harp fumbled head first on the run way that George Sage is headed for. He receives more scrapes and bruises as he stands up and discharges his fifth discharge. He waits bruised and damaged for the field to materialize. He has to kill George Sage. He waits for the force field. It envelopes him. He is damaged but he moves the force field toward the transport. He has to finish his assignment. He bounces the field toward the entrance to the transport.

He has ten minutes to get to him. George Sage has the Wells Crank. It is useless to him but he holds it close to his chest. Harp is on a mission and his assignment is to kill George Sage and Gloria Goldmine. George Sage is just ahead of him. Gloria Goldmine and Brenda are probably on another transport for who knows where. He must kill George Sage. He keeps bouncing down the runway toward the transport that George Sage thinks will allow him to escape from Harp.

Harp keeps bouncing down the runway. He thinks he will be able to kill George Sage easily. He underestimates the enforcer in George Sage. He didn't live this long to die so easily. He waits for Harp at the entrance to the transport. He throws the Wells Crank down the run way toward Harp.

"Now you will die."

Harp doesn't hesitate. He bounces full force at George Sage and sends both of them into the cockpit of the transport. George Sage pushes Harp down. He pushes the buttons that will send the transport into outer space. Harp pins George Sage to the control panel. He is enveloped in the force field though and can't stop him from pushing buttons that will control the transport. Harp looks on as George Sage sends the transport into detector evading mode.

The cockpit is now out of control. George Sage looks into Harp's eyes and laughs.

"Nobody will win today."

He then closes his eyes because he doesn't want to see his death.

The transport begins to maneuver in all sorts of crazy patterns. Harp is thrown all around the cockpit. George Sage's body is thrown around the cockpit like a rag doll in a washing machine. It is torn to pieces after being flung into everything in the cockpit. Harp is safe in his envelope of the force field. He suddenly finds that his force field has disintegrated and he crashes into instruments and the human remains of George Sage. He crawls into a pilots seat and somehow manages to strap himself to it. He activates his homing devise by pushing his eyebrows together. IIA will pick up the signal. Harp is torn and bruised but can't help but wonder what has happened to Brenda and Gloria Goldmine as he passes out.

He goes into rehab again.

"Harp! Can you see me?"

He looks up into the eyes of Miss Perriweather and HMS.

"I guess I lived."

"You are the best!"

"Where is Brenda?"

"Who is Brenda?"

GAMBLER

SETH HAS A PAIR OF 7's with a king high. He stares at Hoffman and knows he has nothing. He raises all in. Hoffman stares at Seth. Seth smiles and licks his lips. Hoffman folds. Hoffman turns over two jacks and then leaves the table. He wouldn't let Seth see how defrocked he felt. Seth has won his bluff. Seth takes his winnings and cashes out. Seth is a gambler. He is not satisfied. It is like he is an addict. Gambling is not just a job, it is his whole life. He goes to his favorite burger joint and pigs out.

Seth is still in debt. A gambler never really wins. They only pay off their losses and return the next day to either win a little money or go into deeper debt . It is a business that the mob and many other people take advantage of. Seth is playing outside of the mob. He only borrows from family and friends. They charge less and they won't kill him. He lives in Vegas though and his reputation as a loser is well known. His family has always gotten the news when he wins. His uncle enters the burger joint and sits down across from him as he is gobbling down his burger and fries.

"You won tonight. You owe and we need something."

Seth stares at his uncle and says, "Can you read my poker face?"

His uncle cold cocks him.

Seth regains consciousness. He is face down in catsup covered french fries. His entire winnings has been taken from his person. He is broke again. So much for family as he is left with only his lucky silver dollar. It is his most cherished possession. A friend of his, Petee, comes to his rescue, pays his bill and helps him out of Big Bob's Burgers.

"Seth you got to change man! Your family will kill you one day."

"I'm already dead. I just want to live to make a bet on when it happens. I'm a gambler."

Seth's eye is bleeding a little and his head hurts. He spends the night on the floor of Petee's apartment, a dump outside of the strip but close enough to walk back to it if you were able. Seth stands up and looks into a mirror in the bathroom and squeezes his eye. It hurts but he has to make the swelling go away. He gets in the shower and turns the water to hot. He has to make his body look like he is a player. He gets out of the shower and wipes off the mirror in the bathroom. His eye is not going to look good for at least another day. He sits on the couch with a towel wrapped around his waist and asks Petee to get him a beer. He understands that this is the fate of gamblers. When you win you are living high. When you lose or have to pay off back debts you will have to dig your way back to the surface. Seth will try to figure out who will front him the money for his next game. Right now he is a mole.

Seth has a girlfriend who works as a barmaid at one of the best casinos. She makes good tips. His face is looking much better after two days. He goes to her for another loan. He owes her several thousand dollars but she really likes him and always seems to help him out when he is scrambling. If he is winning he spends his money buying her things. She is just as much of a fool as he is. She is just as much of a gambler as he is also. She loans him another grand. He kisses her and leaves to find a game. She locks her door and goes to the casino. It is just another day in Vegas.

Seth needs a big win. His face is presentable because he uses makeup. His eye is not functioning at 100% but he is a gambler. He plays at some of the local casinos and makes a few hundred dollars but he needs to get back to the strip. He decides to play craps. He has to get enough money to enter a big stakes game. He walks into the Fool's Gold Casino. It has a no limits craps table. He isn't known there and that is a good thing. He goes to the craps table and waits for his turn to throw the dice. He plays cautiously and is winning a little. His turn to roll comes up. He looks up at the cameras and prays that no one knows him. He starts to bet heavy. He is on a good roll and is about $5000.00 ahead. He looks around. He doubles all his bets, closes his eyes and throws the dice. He rolls a double three. He is now up about $7000.00. He takes his chips and cashes out. He walks out of the casino looking over his shoulders. He is scared. He needs the money though. He gets to his car, opens the door and gets in. He puts the key in the ignition and starts it up. He puts it in reverse, turns the wheels toward the highway and leaves the casino's parking lot. He just might make it back to the strip.

Seth floors his car and never looks back. He is headed for the strip. He has to get into a big game. The Fool's Gold Casino will soon know who he is and will be unhappy that he took them for over $7000.00. They will either come after him or check out who he knows in Vegas. If he is lucky he will get back to the strip and into a big stakes game.

Seth walks into "Poker Heaven."

He gives his money to the cashier, collects his chips, and walks over to the big money poker table. He is ready to gamble and he needs to face the best. He is a gambler. He is about to find out if his family will allow him to live another day. He owes everyone in the family. One of his uncles got some of what he was owed but Seth still owes almost everyone in his family and that means that this might be the last poker game he will ever play if he doesn't win. Seth sits and puts his chips in front of him. He has balls the size of a bull.

"Deal the cards!"

The table is filled with faces a normal gambler wouldn't want to meet head to head. Seth hacks and spits into an empty glass.

"That is just a sample of what you will get out of me!"

He smiles at the table. They look among themselves and tell the dealer to deal the cards. It is Seth's funeral. He is about to play the game of his life. Cell phones start calling his family. He just entered the most important game that he would ever play. He is now just a gamble away from death. The first card he gets is an ace. He lifts the second one and it is a paired deuce. He lets out a sigh. He begins to sweat. The door to the poker room opens and three of his uncles enter. They start talking on their cell phones. Seth has made this a family affair. He is playing for his life. He is playing with family money. They are powerless to help him. He will either win or they will have to make him disappear. Everyone at the table looks to the family to make sure that Seth understands that they aren't bluffing. Seth is playing with the big boys and he is betting his life. His family calls him over.

"Seth these guys don't play games. They are this town. You need more than balls tonight. You owe the family but if you owe these guys it is out of our hands. We forgive but these guys demand payment."

Seth looks his uncles in the eye. "Do I look like a loser to you?"

His family turn their backs to Seth. They walk out of the card room. Seth is now on his own. The family is not playing anymore. It is Seth against the old boys.

Seth sucks in his breath and smiles at the table. "So how about a drink? I am buying."

He could be frozen by the stares that are focused on him. He continues to smile.

"Waitress I would like a beer. In a frozen mug."

He doesn't look at any of the players. They wouldn't be stupid enough to give him a tell this early in the game. He takes his beer and leans forward.

"Is anyone else feeling uncomfortable?"

The cards are turned over. Seth has four spades and a straight draw. A three and five of spades with a ten of hearts.

"All in."

Two players fold. The third player lifts his cards and then folds. It is now Seth and two real monsters. The first one shoves in his chips in. Seth really starts to sweat. The last player shoves in his chips.

Seth grabs his balls. He is all in and has nothing else going for him.

The next card is the king of diamonds.

The first player bets another forty-five hundred. The other player calls. Seth asks for more chips. "I want to bet four thousand more chips."

The players look at each other.

"You know if you cannot pay we will kill you?"

"I bet five thousand dollars. Do you accept my bet?"

They look at each other and shake their heads.

Both accept the bet.

The river card is about to be turned. Seth is sweating and knows he is now the loneliest person in the room. There is no one that will come to his rescue. He either wins or he is dead.

The river card is turned over. It is the eight of clubs.

MORAL TO THIS STORY

Only gamble with your family because everyone else doesn't give a damn.

THE STAR

"WELL, STAN, WHAT DO YOU think?"

"It is hard to tell Frank, but I think he has a fighting chance to pull through. It could have been a lot worse. Do you remember when we had to sew him up when his third wife took to his back with a straight razor after he passed out back in 07? And then there was the time that he jumped off the balcony into his fifth wife's wedding cake? We patched him up then and he healed. I just hope that he has plans to play Evil Kinevil in his next picture or maybe a robot cowboy. At least his scars will blend in with the character until we have finished his next reconstructive surgery. My initial examination has me worried."

"I will admit that he is a mess. He was beaten senseless by champaign bottles that his fourteen year old daughter decided might stop him from trying to have sex with her friends. He was drunk and on drugs and that is the only reason that he was still alive. He doesn't have more than a square foot of un-bruised or broken parts left in his body. I used three feet of suture on him and I might have to put him in a full body cast."

The two doctors stood conferencing with each other outside of a special wing at the hospital that was reserved for only one patient. That patient was Lane Tassel. He had donated so much money to the hospital that it had agreed that he could have his own private section. The doctors were waiting for his personal assistant.

"Stan! Frank! How bad is he?"

"You should probably be asking me if he is still alive? We have him sedated and he is in traction. You won't be able to talk to him for a few hours, if at all, as we had to wire his jaws shut so that we can recon-struct his face. I've been his reconstructive surgeon for nine years and this might be the worst damage that has ever been inflicted to his body. Those girls just kept beating him with those champaign bottles. If his daughter hadn't stopped them then he would be dead. At least she had the decency to call the paramedics before going clubbing"

The threesome headed for the kitchen in the Lane Tassel wing of the hospital.

Florence Gail Heath Tassel had been Lane's per-sonal assistant for ten years now. He called her "Flo." That was her Lane Tassel name. Once he gave you a name that was the only name you had in his presence. She had even been foolish enough to marry him once. She did love him though and could not remember a dull moment in her life since he said, "Gal, I like your spirit! How would you like to ball a movie star?"

They entered the kitchen upbeat, which was really quite remarkable since they had the responsibility of keeping the Lane Tassel of stage, television, and screen alive and capable of producing one mega hit after another for the last ten or so years alive. Lane was everything and more that a modern idol could be. He was in his performances, as in life, what only most people could dream about. He had charisma mixed with bad karma, but he also had a special magic that people couldn't ignore even if they tried. He was the most talented and self destructive performer to arrive on the show-biz scene in over a decade. They would now have to create the Frankenstein Monster again out of what was left of his damaged and bruised body. They were the only people on the planet that truly knew what Lane was, a mass of highly successful operations and a true wonder in the field of reconstructive surgery. He had managed to finish 16 movies in 10 years which was an amazing feat because he had been in hospitals or recovery rooms for about a third of that time. He and they would have to perform another miracle because he was due in Spain on the 24th of October to play the role of a young Picasso, then on to Colorado to do a western. They poured themselves a cup of coffee and seated themselves. They were in for a marathon.

"I have a new method of reducing scar tissue and we have enough of his skin to graft over the rest of his older scars so that he will be presentable in about two to three weeks. I have a new light treatment and some chemical baths that might speed up the healing, but it all depends upon Lane."

Flo threw her hands in the air.

"What am I supposed to do now?"

"You are one in a million. You have sacrificed your life for Lane just to keep him on top of the world. There is only one "Lane Tassel" and you are the only person that can save him. I can rebuild him, but you have to make him want to be the Lane Tassel that everyone loves. I hope you want to?"

Flo walked over to a corner of the kitchen.

" I am just about done with him. I have had to rebuild his ego after each of his incidents. I wish I had your job. Do you want to switch places?"

"Not on your life! I wouldn't take your job for all the money in the world. I don't need a star to shine his light on me. I just make him get up and do it again."

Flo lowered her head. She was tired. Ten years of making Lane an idol was wearing on her. She needed a break. She had made plans for a vacation. She was going to replace herself with a new assistant. She picked up her cell phone and made a call.

The three of them left the kitchen and headed toward the room that Lane was recovering in. It had a star on the door and that star was supposed to be Lane. They opened the door.

"It is very bright in here. Put on these googles. They will protect your eyes from the light treatments. We are spraying his body with chemical baths that promote healing. He has been undergoing these treatments since we brought him into this room. I am scared. These treatments are making him aggressive."

Flo looked into Lane's eyes. He stared back at her like a tiger on a leash.

"Get out of here!"

Everyone left the room.

It had been a week since Flo had visited him at the hospital. She entered Lane's room and turned off all of the instruments. She released him from his restraints.

"Lane you promised me that if I released you that you wouldn't hurt me."

"You have this coming Flo."

He chased her around the room until he cornered her. He tore her clothes from her body and pleasured himself with her as many times as he could. Flo was pleasantly surprised. She had forgotten how good sex could be with Lane. Lane was more than a movie star, he was a sexual pervert. She knew that his aggressive sexual ability was just due to the treatments that Stan and Frank had used on him. She left the room. She had hired her replacement. She covered herself and left the hospital. She was done with Lane. She was going on a vacation for the first time in ten years. She hoped that she would never have to come back. She handed Frank a note as she left. It read. "She is my replacement. Trust me! She can do the job. Lane needs her. I cannot deal with him anymore. I am going on a lifetime vacation. Have fun with Lane in the future." Flo closed her eyes and walked away from the hospital. She had just sentenced her sister to Hell.

PATTI

Patti Frost scanned the directory on the first floor of the hospital. She had never been to a hospital that catered to mainly the super rich. She was going to meet Lane Tassel and she would be working for him. Flo left her with Lane. She was now not just a wannabe. Her career as an actress ended here. She was now Lane Tassel's personal assistant. She was also Flo's sister. Flo was leaving Lane to her. She didn't know what she was getting into. Flo wanted out and dumped Lane on her. She would either learn how to take care of him or he would die and the world would lose Lane. Patti entered the elevator that would take her to Lane's personal wing of the hospital. She was going to meet his doctors. Flo had told her that they would be needed constantly. Lane was a destructive personality. He wanted to die everyday but he had to finish each movie first. Lane needed a reason to wake up each morning. He needed a movie to star in. That was Patti's new job. She had to make Lane Tassel want to wake up.

THE DOCTORS

"So you must be Patti?"

"Welcome to behind the scenes."

"Dr. Parker or Hamm?"

"Neither, it is Stan to you if you are the new Flo."

"Why so personal?"

"If you are going to take your sister's place even for a short period of time, then you need to get used to calling people by their Lane name. The Lane Tassel name."

"Okay Stan, so what are you talking about?"

"Lane calls people whatever he wants to. If they stick around for a while that is who they become. They become who Lane thinks they are. That is the power of Lane Tassel."

"I thought my sister was just kidding me about this world of his? So how do I control this crazy son of a bitch?"

"Don't take anything too seriously around here. If you do then you will not have a soul or a heart worth saving in less time than it takes for to you to ask "how did I get here and how can I get out of this place."

"In other words, Flo escaped by making me Lane's keeper?"

"She sold you to the devil, so to speak."

"Lane Tassel is supposed to be my master then?"

"Flo paid many prices to keep him alive. He is a destructive personality. He wants to die on camera, but if it doesn't happen, then he will try it off camera. Flo made sure that didn't happen. Now it is your job."

"So I am supposed to keep a suicidal maniac from becoming front page news?"

"No, you are supposed to keep Lane Tassel in the news, He must remain a star."

"Our job is to repair him after he self destructs. I am Frank. Frank Hamm in the real world. Frank in Lane's world."

"Flo never told me that I would become a nursemaid."

"Flo needed to get away. She must have thought you could handle Lane and keep him alive. We have for at least the last ten years with her help. We have become very wealthy because of his antics. He should have died many times. We found ways to recreate what he destroyed. We have written medical journals on recovery from his supposedly fatal wounds. We performed them and made a fortune by using his reconstructive surgery procedures. He is special to us. Keep him safe."

"So Lane Tassel recovering from life threatening antics is what you care about?"

"No, Lane Tassel in the news keeps us in the business of making beautiful people. We are New York and Hollywood. We make beautiful people. Lane is our poster boy."

"Plastic surgeons? So you are now going to tell us what we are supposed to look like in the future?"

"No, Lane Tassel has to remain a star or all of us will be out of a job. Your job is to make him want to be that star. Flo gave you her job. It is now up to you to take her place."

Patti stood outside the recovery room trying to gain the courage to enter it.

How she was supposed to react or what she was to about to see wasn't what anyone in her position could plan for. She didn't have a clue as to how she was going to face Lane. She was more scared than anytime in her life. She had only imagined meeting Lane Tassel in her dreams, but meeting him in person was not ever a reality to her. Now she was supposed to take care of him and keep him making movies. She was even sort of related to him. She sucked in her gut and opened the door to her meeting Lane Tassel and her future. Flo had given her a ticket into the light fantastic. She was now Lane Tassel's handler.

Lane was standing in front of a full length mirror.

"Who are you?"

"Oh, I guess you weren't expecting me? Didn't Flo tell you that I would be your traveling companion for your next few movies?"

Lane looked at Patti with lust in his eyes.

"Your doctors told me that you are on very aggressive sexual drugs so I brought a cattle prod to make you pay attention to your recovery. I am Flo's sister Patti. You can call me Miss Frost."

She punched Lane with the cattle prod. He collapsed on the floor.

"Just who in Hell do you think you are?"

"I am your body guard for at least the Spain trip. I was hired by Flo to make sure that you don't damage yourself again. I take my job seriously and I need this job."

Lane studied her.

"I hope that Flo told you that I was again a divorced man and I don't need much coaxing to get to know. How about you and me getting to know each other better before we have to board that plane for Spain?"

"Well, since you already seem to be in love with the full length mirror, then I shouldn't be needed till flight time."

Patti walked out of the room blushing. Lane was an amazing man and he definitely was a star. She sucked in her breath. Patti couldn't help but speak out loud.

"How in the world am I going to control the star?"

ALWAYS FOLLOW YOUR LEADER

"MAY I TALK TO YOU Millie?"

"Sure Carl, as a matter of fact I think that we need to talk."

"I have been afraid to talk to you about some things that have been happening to me for fear that you would think that I was crazy. I want you to listen to me and then make some sort of judgement. Will you listen to me?"

"Yes, I will listen to you."

"I can't be sure that all that has been happening to me is real or is just something that my mind has concocted. It all started when I began writing my thesis on mysticism. I know this might seem to be insanity but something or someone is trying to control my thoughts. I have spent more than three years doing research on various superstitions and folklore that have been known to be connected to Satanism. I have visited various sites that were claimed to be haunted. I visited the pyramids in Egypt. I even visited many pagan sites in Europe. Now, would you believe that so far none of these places revealed any proof that an evil entity existed at any point in history, yet people still believe in the Devil. I just returned from Salem, Massachusetts where witches were supposedly being raised. There is no proof that the Devil existed there as far as my research can prove. But since I have been trying to explain what I have discovered in my research, all sorts of weird things have been happening. I have been locked in rooms that couldn't possibly be locked unless something supernatural locked them. Every time I try to set an appointment to finish my thesis paper the phone either goes dead or turns to static. Now the worst part is that everything I say or do has a strange effect upon people. I also seem to have people following me. I know this may sound like an acute state of paranoia, but believe me, these people are real. I saw an old indian following me the other day that could have been one of the brujos that I studied on a visit to the ancient ruins in Mexico. The other day a man that seemed to be European was following me. I approached him and he just disappeared as if he was never there. I am beginning to wonder if anything that I see is real or is just an illusion that someone wants me to see. Please, you need to help me understand what is happening to me."

"Ok Carl, but first you must understand a few

things about me. I am a witch that grew up in Salem. I was given the task of watching you and reporting to my coven what you were researching. You have been medalling in areas that the coven doesn't want to be discovered. You either must stop your thesis or be forced to join us in our secrecy. This will be the only warning you will be given. You are being watched very closely. You just don't know how powerful the forces are that are following your every move now. You are researching the Devil, but you have found everyone else."

Carl shook his head. "So I wasn't just imagining things? They were real."

Carl looked at Millie and laughed.

"You can't be a witch, or can you be one?"

"Do you think our meeting was by chance? I was ordered to meet you and cast a spell on you. I never thought mortals were so intelligent as to not become pawns to our spells. You seem to be immune to my spells. I have cast many and you still seem to just shuck them off. My sisters and brothers in the coven also wonder what makes you so special?"

"So what you are saying is that my reality is just a dream?"

"No, I am saying that you are not normal. I was told to tell you that the coven is looking at you as some sort of a mutant. You seem to be immune to our spells. You scare us."

"Witches and their cohorts! You think all men

are just tools. Remember, males rule the world, females just control it. You need a male or you are just a beast that walks upon the earth with no purpose. Males have desires and must exercise them. We will still find some way to exist."

Millie wasn't sure what to say. She was a witch. Carl was asking her to believe in a person that she never thought about before. She shook her head and spoke.

"You are trying to confuse me. What have you and the Devil got to do with witches?"

Carl laughed hard and long.

"My research into satanism was just my way of keeping you interested in me. What do you really feel about me?"

Millie stepped back. She wasn't really sure of how she felt about Carl. He was always just a subject she was to report to the coven about.

"Millie, you can cast spells and even make a person not know where or what they did at some point in their life, but can you be real?"

Millie shook her head. Carl was making her feel crazy.

"Who are you?"

"You want me to accept the circle of witches and your coven. You expect me to understand that you can cast spells on humans that control them.. I do."

"Carl I can't understand you. You go against everything that I have ever been taught. You are more of a mystery to me than my powers. I have made mortals crawl at my feet and beg for mercy. I have made priests throw away their vows and stab themselves with crosses. I have been alive for many lifetimes of a normal human, yet you seem to mock me. You are not religious and don't seem to worship any god. What are you?"

"If what you say is true then I am the one who is in control. Even your so called all powerful circle can't control me. This means that I am their master. The ultimate male, the only male that can control the women that control."

"Carl, you are just a mortal. Mortals can't exist in our world. Our lifespan is three or four times that of a human. You cannot rule where you will perish in less than a third of our lifetime. You will perish and the circle will continue."

Carl laughed again very hard and long. He stares at Millie and then confronts her with a dare.

"You are about to show me my power over you. You say that I can't cast an illusion. Cast an illusion."

Millie didn't know what to do. She cast an illusion.

"There, I cast an illusion."

"You tricked me."

"No, I cast an illusion. You just did it for me."

"Carl you are in danger. The circle will kill you. They know about you because of me."

"So, you are now an outcast in the circle because you didn't kill me."

"I am so confused. You are making me crazy. I don't know what to do?"

"If I promise to take care of you then you must be loyal to only me. The circle of witches will have to answer to me. Are you ready to trust only in me?"

"Carl, I am afraid. If I defy the circle then I am sure both of us will perish."

Carl laughed out loud again.

"Millie, I am a mortal that has captured a witch. What else can happen to you?"

"I promise that I will be loyal to only you. I am now yours and yours only."

At this statement Carl screams into the sky.

"I dare the darkness to show itself to me. I will become your master. I now have Millie as mine."

Lightning and thunder filled the sky around Millie and Carl. Carl just laughs and yells to the sky.

"Is that all you have?"

Out of nowhere witches and warlocks emerge as if summoned by the Devil himself.

"The witch Millie has now become an outcast. She as well as you will pay for defying the circle."

"So, you think that because your magicians and your so called religious priests that controlled the world for centuries can keep you in control?"

"Are you ready to die Mortal?"

Carl belts out a laugh again and brings Millie out in front of him.

"I now have Millie and I think we can make a stand."

"No mortal can withstand our powers. You and your witch will perish this day."

Carl makes Millie look into his eyes.

"Now is the time that I will need your powers. If you really do belong to me then you must trust in only me. Can you follow your leader?"

Millie stares into Carl's eyes.

"I am yours and yours only."

"Powers of evil! Guardians of the night and the protectors of the circle come to our aid." The war-locks and witches begin chanting together.

Carl leads Millie to an area and makes a circle with his foot. They enter the circle and stand back to back. Carl then tells Millie to make the circle a ring of fire. Millie does so without any hesitation. Carl turns and kisses her. He then yells at the witches and warlocks.

"If you refuse to obey me then my witch will prove to you that your magic and illusions are just that. You cannot defeat us. She is my power now."

"We demand that you surrender your witch to us. No one can defeat the circle. We have powers that cannot be stopped."

A flood of water starts rushing toward Carl's ring of fire. Carl tells Millie to shut her eyes and concentrate on the ring of fire. He laughs as the water just rushes around the ring of fire.

"My witch is very powerful. Bring on your next illusion."

The circle did what Carl expected them to do. They tried an aerial attack.

Carl tells Millie to raise the ring of fire. They float in the ring of fire above the circle. The vulture type creatures that have been sent are burned and fall to the ground. Carl again laughs at the circle members.

"My witch is powerful. Show me what Hell has to offer. So far a mortal and a captured witch seem to have gained an edge!"

Carl instructs Millie to lower them back to the circle that he had made with his foot. She didn't hesitate. Carl is her master. She will follow him to Hell if he asked her to.

Carl screams at the circle members.

"So, you thought that it would be simple to kill me and my witch. She seems to be more than you thought she was. Can a mere mortal and a witch defeat the great circle?"

"Mortal!"

One of the circles members voice hissed.

"You will perish and your witch will feel the damnation of the circle. Be prepared for Hell. We have been alive for centuries and will continue long after you are dead."

Carl again laughs so loud as to make an echo.

"You boast that you are immortal. I think my witch is better than you. She doesn't care about you anymore. She only wants to follow my lead. She will only follow her leader and I am him."

At this the circle amasses a wall of blood. They send it toward the circle that Carl and Millie have made. Carl instructs Millie to enter the wall and confront the circle. Millie and Carl escape the goo of blood and face the members of the circle.

"Master! Master! We thought you were just a mortal. Please have mercy upon us."

Carl looks at Millie.

"You have proven to me that you are loyal."

He then transforms himself into the Devil that he truly is. He laughs loud and hard at the circle members. He turns to Millie. His eyes are glowing dark red. His body ignites into flames.

"Millie you have been tested and have passed the test. You remained loyal to only me. Now as the "King of Darkness" I take this witch as my queen."

At this statement Millie disintegrates and then becomes flames. She is now the "Queen of Darkness."

EMOTION

27 MONTHS! HOW MUCH LONGER could he take it? Roger could not tell anyone what was happening to him. They would think that he had fallen into a state of insanity. His friends were beginning to think that he was crazy. His family considered him a stranger. Roger knew what was tormenting him and he tried many times to tell someone, anyone, what he had seen on that night that made him one of loneliest people on the planet. He lost every old friend that he had and now his family was ready to disown him. He was being judged by everyone as very strange. He was a prisoner, of what, only he knew.

27 months ago Roger went on a vacation to Yellowstone National Park. He decided to climb up the Grand Tetons and camp on top of them if he could. He could not get any of his friends to go along on the attempt, but Paul Williams, Frank Smith, Joan Layton, and Steve and Lonnie Wilcox said that they would

camp at the base of the Tetons and promised to keep a telescope on his climb. They lost site of him on the third day and had no visual site of him after a week. They informed the rangers at the park that they were fearful that something happened to him. That night he wandered into their camp and collapsed. He was physically and mentally exhausted and fell into what turned out to be a three day sleep. He never was the same after that vacation. His friends gave up wondering what happened to him on that climb. Roger decided that he needed to face his adversary or he would truly go insane.

Roger was living like a hermit. He, during the months after returning to Boston had become a person that slept at weird hours when he could and only ate when someone made him. He was constantly in a state of daydreaming and could not do his job. He was sent home on sick leave. He was soon let go and could not get anyone else to hire him. He became the talk of the town. He was a man that had lost his sanity in Yellowstone National Park. That was what made him decide to return to the Tetons. He had to face the creature that was making his life a nightmare. He could only return to his old friends and family after he faced this creature that was keeping him in a state of insanity. He would once again climb the mountain alone. This time no one would be watching, that is unless the creature was?

Roger could not possibly explain to anyone that

he discovered a creature on his climb that took over his mind and haunted him constantly. They would never believe him. He would seem like a mad man. It didn't matter anymore though as he was a mad man. The creature made him one. It called to him constantly and he could not escape it's callings. He had to go back and face it. He needed to know why he was chosen. The creature was not from this earth, or at least it didn't seem to be. He tried to drink the creature out of his mind. He stayed awake for days in hopes that it was just a dream. The creature was just there. It kept calling to him. He had no choice but to go back and face it.

Roger took a bus to Yellowstone and only brought his climbing equipment and a tape recorder with him. If he found the creature then he wanted to record what it had to say. The problem was that it never spoke to him. He only heard it calling to him in his mind. He remembered the first time that he met the creature. He tried to flee from it, but it flew ahead of him and made his attempts at escape impossible. It never really threatened him. It just kept him where it could control his movements. It finally chased him down and flew away with him in its grasp to its nest. He remembered being fondled and stroked constantly by it. It even tried to give him a bread like substances to feed upon. He remembered that after several days of starving himself the creature flew with him and let him go free near his friend's campsite. That was where Roger was supposed to get back to his life, only the creature never really released him. It was still in his mind, calling to him.

Roger found the site where he first started his climb all those months ago. He felt peaceful. He decided to climb until he reached the creature's nest. He was sure that he remembered the area where it was located. He was wrong. The creature had been hidden from this world for so many years because it had a hidden site for its nest. He climbed relentlessly and finally got to a point where he was exhausted. He collapsed. The next thing he knew was that he was flying. The creature found him and was taking him to its nest. Roger was ready to accept the creature and its nest. He was mentally tired and now had to understand what the creature wanted with him?

The creature slowly lowered itself to where it placed Roger in its nest. As soon as the creature got close to him, Roger leaped at it and brought it down with him. He had new strength and would overpower it if he could. Suddenly, with incredible ease, the creature escaped his grasp and floated above him. It didn't seem to want to harm him. It seemed to be studying him. It wasn't that hideous looking. In fact it was magnificent. It was not like anything he had ever seen before. It had human characteristics yet it had wings that were very shiny and flexible. Its body was very pink and smooth looking. It was completely hairless, but when he was struggling with it he noticed that it was covered with what he could only explain as a fluffy substance. It made it look larger than it was because of it. He overpowered it easily as it could only weigh about a hundred pounds. It did have incredible speed though and that was why it had escaped from him so easily. It just floated above him looking down at him with what seemed like moon eyes.

The creature began to motion for Roger to join it. He was not sure what was going on. He rose to his feet and decided to try and communicate with it.

"What do you want from me?"

It moved closer to him and for the first time he didn't want to flee from it. He asked again.

"What do you want from me? Why do you want me to come to you?"

The creature lowered itself into the nest and started caressing him. It stroked him like a newborn baby. He became afraid and tried to escape. The creature moved with such speed that Roger was left with no escape. Roger then got a mental picture from the creature. It was too jumbled for him to understand. He screamed.

"What do you want?"

The creature opened what was its mouth and spoke.

"I----------------for--------------you."

The creature kept trying to speak and finally

Roger understood what it was trying to say. "I am not here to harm but for to help. Need you."

Roger looked up. The creature was about three feet from him. He was guessing that it was trying to learn how to speak to him. He was only getting mental pictures from it.

"You need to tell me what you want?"

The creature landed beside him and began caressing him again. He let it. He then asked again.

"What do you want from me?"

The creature hugged him and said in a very strange voice.

"You. I, need you."

"Make sense! What am I here for?"

"I am alone."

Roger understood that. He yanked himself away from the creature and tried to run.

The creature moved with incredible speed and cut him off. Roger stood still and stared at the creature.

It spoke.

"I showed you how to feel lonely."

"Why do you want me to come with you?"

"I am Pylot. I am the last of my kind."

"What is a Pylot?"

"Pylot is we. We is now I."

"Where are the rest of the Pylots?"

"There are no more. I am Pylot."

Roger now understood what this creature

wanted. It was the last of its kind. It was looking for a mate. He wasn't sure that he wanted to be used by this creature. He only knew that for over two years it had tortured him into returning to it. He thought about what his life had become. He could never go back to his old life. Maybe he really was destined to become the creature's mate. He opened his arms and let the creature stroke him. He could never go back to Boston.

THE SESSION

"HAROLD BANNISTER, CARD NUMBER 0196876. three nights a week with Dr. Morris."

The door opened and Harold entered the first room of his group education class. Feeling orbs arose before him. As usual Harold went to the medium orb and began his tactile test. He reacted just as he had reacted for most of his sessions. He began to react to the tingling sensation that resulted from the programed sexual desires. Dr. Ibis had to interrupt Harold's fantasy to get him into phase two, the inhibition chamber. His image appeared on a screen as Harold was fulfilling his sexual desires upon the orb.

"Harold, you must move on to the inhibition chamber."

Harold quit his business with the orb and moved on to the door that would lead him into the next phase of understanding where he stood in society.

Harold understood that this therapy was required for a person of his skill level.

Harold was success programed. He was eager to cooperate with this session because several positions were now available in his field in higher skill levels. He wanted to prove that he was willing to do whatever was necessary to be given a higher skill level. He was a skill level of just fifty-fifty. That meant he was programed to either rise or fall in society depending upon these sessions..

Harold was Dr. Ibis's pet because he was the easiest to monitor and control. That is why he was given the first position in the group. He could be rushed through the tests without any variations each time he was there. Harold was now going to be programed to hate where he was in society. He entered phase two, the inhibition chamber.

"Gertrude Mathis, card number 100345, two nights a week with Dr. Morris."

The door opened and again the orbs arose in front of her. Gertrude went to orb one, the smallest orb. This was normal for her. She was a skill level seventy-five. This meant that there were going to be very few positions in her field that would become available for her to become a higher skill level. She passed over the orb with very little excitement. She was used to actual human touch and was even married to a skill level eighty. She was allowed to enter into the next chamber without Dr. Ibis having to show his image on the entrance screen. She was with child thus given the number two position in the group.

"Stanley Veeber, card number 056789, three nights a week with Dr. Morris."

He entered the room and again the orbs arose in front of him. He went to orb one, then to orb two, and then to orb three. He was not ready to give his superiors control over his feelings. Stanley was a skill level sixty which meant he was not yet classified to become available for a position in management but was under consideration to apply for a position there.

He would remain a skill level sixty until this group education session could determine where his skills could be effectively used in society. He was given position number three because he was the most unpredictable in the group that had been selected for this session. He went into phase two without any hesitation because he would do whatever came natural to him. He entered without fear of who he was. Dr. Ibis's image just smiled as he entered the door to phase two.

"Nancy Bean, card number 009076, one night a week with Dr. Morris."

Nancy is a psychiatrist. She is only required to come to the session one night a week to help determine how the group is comparing with the other groups. She is only interested in how this group is maintaining a balance between the higher and lower skill levels in society. She and position five are the levels that Dr. Ibis needs for his weekly evaluation reports. They are skill level eighty-five and above and therefore he needs them to be his apprentices. She was given position four to make the last two positions available for her to make her weekly assessment. She bypasses the orbs and enters the next phase while Dr. Ibis looks on from his visual screen.

"William Post, card member 000987, six nights a week with Dr. Morris."

William is a ninety in skill level evaluations. He is the first of his kind to maybe reach a level one hundred skill level. This makes him second in command to Dr. Ibis. He is here six nights a week to supervise the session and possibly take over for Dr. Ibis in the future. He is required to meet with this group six nights a week to gain the experience he will need to take over future sessions.

He is not in the session for treatment, but for education. Dr. Ibis has to make sure that no matter what, this session has to be completed for the evaluation board. William is keeping records that will be compared with all the failed sessions that Dr. Morris and the other computers have recorded. He was given position five in case Dr. Ibis needed someone to be present in an emergency. He needs someone present to be his strong-arm in case the session becomes unmanageable. He walks by the orbs and enters phase two. Dr. Ibis just looks on from his screen.

"Ian Foster, card member 097654, three nights a week with Dr. Morris."

Ian entered the room and immediately began to strip. He attacks the orbs in no order. He will not ever be able to have sexual relations with another human. He is a level fifty-fifty which means he might do anything and he does so each time he comes to a session. He is allowed to release his built up frustrations on the orbs. He is given all the time that he needs to get to a stable mind set to enter into phase two. He is a lost cause which makes him perfect for the sixth position in this session. Dr. Ibis just looks down from his screen as William enters the door to phase two.

"Howard McDoyle, card member 127432, five nights a week with Dr. Morris."

Howard is a forty skill level. He isn't retarded, he just has a mental block against becoming responsible for his actions. He is a follower. He enters the room and hesitates before the orbs that grow before him. He touches one of the orbs and becomes so ashamed that he collapses. Dr. Ibis looks down from his screen. He speaks to Howard.

"You must go into the door to phase two."

Howard stands up and shuffles toward the door that will lead him to phase two. He is perfect for the number seven position in this session.

"Betty Ormis, card member 111345, five nights a week with Dr. Morris."

Betty can not be classified on any skill level because she is not cooperating and all of the tests that determine what skill level that a patient should be evaluated in the controlled society are not working on her. She enters the room and begins destroying the orbs. She avoids any sensations that the orbs can record about her. She shoots her finger at the image of Dr. Ibis and enters phase two. She is the prize patient that Dr. Ibis needs to make the session the most remarkable of any in history. She just needs to be made to understand that he is in control.

"Dr. Morris, card member 000000, a machine that records each word of every member in this session."

He was made to record the session. That is his only purpose. He moves toward the door that leads to phase two. Dr. Ibis lets his visual image disintegrate. He is moving on.

Dr. Ibis comes up on a visual screen that is one wall of the session room. This has been proven to be the best method of letting the society that Dr. Ibis is trying to control understand what is going to become the norm.

This is Dr. Ibis's last session. He has evaluated all the sessions that have been performed in the last twenty-three years. He has a replacement candidate in the group. The session is classical. If his monitor Dr. Morris can get each member of the session to agree to a skill level then he will be the first to make a session successful.

His image comes up on the wall.

"Well it is good to see everyone here. How did the mental tests go in phase two? You can answer first Harold. We will go in order tonight."

"I feel that I can handle a promotion. The strain of moving up to a sixty skill level does not scare me anymore. I used to feel that I could not relate to the people and the daily mind probes but now I feel that it would be a desired change from the fifty-two skill level position that I am now in. I also feel that I can now have tactile sensations with humans instead of orbs. I think that I am even beginning to like people. I talked with a skill level sixty today and she seemed to be friendly. I know it may seem strange but I even told the inhibition phase that I wanted it to shut itself off. I then moved on to phase three without waiting for an answer."

"Very good Harold. Very good indeed. Now how will you handle this new outlook on your life tomorrow?"

"I will talk to this skill level sixty tomorrow. I may even try to touch her, that is if she lets me."

"Very good. Now aren't you happier about your place in this world? Don't you feel that you belong among people again?"

"I am starting to and I thank you and this session."

"Okay, now Gertrude it is your chance to tell us how you feel."

"Well the baby is is starting to kick and Paul got

elevated to a skill level eighty. I don't have to wonder if we will be able to keep our baby. With his promotion we will be allowed to keep our baby. I bless this day and want the session people to know that there is a future."

Dr. Morris rolled across the room and asked. "Do you want to have this baby?"

Gertrude answered.

"I want to have this baby!"

Dr. Morris moved to a position at the other end of the room.

Dr. Ibis stared down at the group from his video picture.

"Now, Stanley how did your phase two go?"

"Not so well. It started attacking me about how I was not capable of assuming a decent skill level. It then told me that I was too lazy to to give up the tactile orbs for human contact. It attacked my manhood. It made me think that all I was capable of copulating with was a forty skill level. I was embarrassed."

Dr. Ibis looked at Stanley from his screen.

"So, what do you think that you are capable of?"

"I am scared. I was experiencing a wake up call. I was being attacked about my manhood. I was being told that I was only capable of having sex with a skill level forty. Do you think I am only capable of having sex with a skill level forty?"

"It is not what I think that counts. What you have to do is to find out what you think. You are not a seventy or even close to a seventy-five skill level. If you don't apply soon then you may never reach a better level."

"I am only going to tell you what most seventy-five and above skill levels know. You will never be a seventy-five skill level or above until you believe that you are superior. You must think that all life-forms are inferior to you. You rule this world. Think about your skill level."

"Now Nancy, how is your schooling coming along?"

"Very well. Your session is making making a big dent in my courses. It will make me a ninety skill level if it is successful. I have reported that our session is ready to be compared with all the failed sessions."

"So the failure rate is still one hundred per cent."

"Yes. I think that I am ready for a ninety and above skill level partner. I need more."

"I hear you. So, how about you William?"

"I have found that you have the best success of all the psychiatrists in these sessions. I am blessed to be in this session. I am proud that you chose me to be your apprentice."

"Well, continue to take notes. Your future will be to make all of the sessions successful."

"Now, how about you Ian?"

"Well I lost my skill level today because I tried to touch a level eighty-five or above. I was fired because I broke all of the security precautions. God! She was so beautiful that I could not resist trying to get her attention. Does beauty come when you become a ninety skill level or above?"

"Not exactly Ian but if you become a ninety skill level you can become whatever you wish. Remember that only five per cent can make it to a ninety level. It is a very important level. It is reserved for the few that can control daylight or darkness for the rest of the planet. So, how will you live in total darkness?"

"I don't know. I attacked the orbs more aggressively than I have ever before. The inhibition tests made me so angry that I had to beat my head against a wall until I couldn't make a fist anymore. I was furious. I lost all control"

"Okay, tell Dr. Morris that you are sorry and will take a fifty-two position in security to make up for your attack."

"I am sorry that I broke through security but I wanted everyone to see that I was more than a sixty skill level. I am very sorry but I can no longer just be satisfied with tactile orbs. I need human contact. I will work in security to make up for my behavior."

Dr. Morris came to Ian. Ian grabbed him.

"Relax Ian, you don't have to touch Dr. Morris. Dr. Morris is not used to being touched. He is just a machine that takes down any conversation that a patient in a session gives. Release him and let him record your words."

"I want a sixty skill level or above. I promise that I will not attack a higher level again."

"Howard, how are you tonight?"

"I am the same. I didn't do anything at all today. I sat in total darkness and didn't care that my machines didn't need anyone to make sure that they were working properly. I might have some cleaning up to do tomorrow but today I just did nothing. I enjoyed the darkness. It made me feel safe."

"Howard, why don't you try to come into the daylight? You could apply for a fifty-fifty skill level position. In fact you could apply for Ian's old position. Just think, you could see real people everyday instead of only in these sessions."

"I like being in the darkness and I don't mind being classified as a forty skill level. It is not like I couldn't do the job of a fifty plus. It is just that I don't mind the total darkness. It makes me feel comfortable."

"Howard, you have got wake up to the controlled world. Do you understand that we are giving you the chance to rise above the forty skill level position? You are a test case for the rest of the fifty per cent that are living in total darkness. Come into the light. This session is your way to find daylight."

"I'm sorry. I just wasn't thinking. I guess I could try the fifty-fifty position and see what daylight is all about. I never really thought about what people see. I can't judge the daylight until I see it. I have only seen machines my whole life and now I guess I can see what people look like. I never saw anyone until I was made to come to this session. I am open to becoming a person in daylight. I want to try to see something besides darkness."

Dr. Morris took his confession and proceeded to the next person in the session.

"OK, now it is your tun. Betty what can you add to this session?"

"Look! I'm only here because you and your fellow computers won't let me live like a human being. What do I have to do to get a job like yours? I bet that you couldn't feel real flesh if you dreamed of it. I even wonder if you aren't just a bunch of circuits like your pot bellied Dr. Morris here."

At this point she kicks Dr. Morris and he falls down.

"This sick bunch of lunatics that you are saying are a part of the real world are just a joke. I see what is going on. Half of this so called controlled world lives in darkness and the other fifty per cent are given daylight only if you control them. These sessions are nothing more than traps. If I wasn't so against them I would go into the darkness and forget that there was such a thing as daylight. If you want me to contribute anything to this session, then it would to make it another failure. That way maybe whatever you and your kind are will come out from from behind those vision screens and mingle with the people that you seem to think that you need to control. Can't you see that hiding behind those screens just prolongs the darkness and leads more people toward it. All this talk of skill levels? What you and the other screen people are saying in these sessions is that to become a one hundred skill level means that you have to leave humans behind and become a machine."

Betty goes over to the corner of the session room and rips the camera that is Dr. Ibis and crushes it under her foot. Dr. Ibis's voice is still audible.

"Betty you shouldn't have done that. Now you will have to be made to understand the one hundred skill levels. The rest of the session is allowed to go."

Every one exists except Betty. She stands in the middle of the room.

"I have made this session another failure. It will be the last failed session because there will be no more."

She had done what no other human that remembered the world before the sessions could do.

She remained human. She would not be controlled by a machine and made to feel, act, and cater to them. She stood up to the one hundred skill level computers. Betty was a real scientist. She created the first one hundred level computer. She programed this computer to talk, emit a human form on a camera, and to feel human tactile sensations through orbs. She helped to give control of all of the weapons and energy to the one hundred level computers during the war. The war destroyed most of the planet. Betty became the student. Her one hundred skill level computer had been running the world for twenty-three years. Betty waited to join a session until the world was once again stabilized under human control. She was now about to destroy the one hundred skill level computers. She turned toward the door that would lead her to the computers. Everyone else had left the underground facilities. Betty now realized that she was just another animal that her one hundred skill level computer needed to control. She was ahead of the computer because she had what no computer could ever have, she could change her mind. She was not controlled by only what memory was programed into its core.

"Dr. Ibis, now that you have found out that there are still some of us that remember before we gave you control of the planet. What will we do? Your selective breeding is very effective but only ten per cent of the population is involved. You didn't know what was going on in the rest of the world which you called darkness. You didn't remember that it was a human that created you and that humans can not be made to cater to their own creations. That is why there was a darkness in your world. We were hiding our children and began making the world like it was before the war. We gave you control of the world to see if you could make it better. We now know that you can't make a better world. You treat humans as if they are just animals and if they have a heart you want to destroy it. I helped to create you and I must now destroy you. We are taking back control of the world."

Betty walks over to the exit and begins her walk toward the computer center. She knows that Dr. Ibis has no eyes on her. She had programed him twenty-three years ago. She took out his eyes in the room that he was supposed to make the first successful session. She walks into a controlled temperature room and looks at the computers she created twenty-three years earlier. Dr. Morris follows her into the area where the computers are stored. They are fifty feet underground. She turns toward Dr. Morris and takes a devise from her pocket. She pushes a button and Dr. Morris fizzles and then goes motionless. She turns toward the computers.

"You, in twenty-three years were given the chance to make a better world. You tried to make humans into computers. Thank you one hundred skill level computer. You have given us the knowledge we needed to create new computers. We are not you."

Betty then played with the gadget she had brought with her and the computer room began smoking from the fried circuits that she was creating. She walked toward the surface of the planet.